LOWER!
HIGHER!
YOU'RE A
LIAR!

A CHARLOTTE ZOLOTOW BOOK
CZ

Miriam Chaikin

LOWER!
HIGHER!
YOU'RE A
LIAR!

Drawings by Richard Egielski

1 8 ⊞ 1 7
———— HARPER & ROW, PUBLISHERS ————
Cambridge, Philadelphia, San Francisco, London, Mexico, City, São Paulo, Sydney
———— NEW YORK ————

Lower! Higher! You're a Liar!
Text copyright © 1984 by Miriam Chaikin
Illustrations copyright © 1984 by Richard Egielski
All rights reserved. No part of this book may be
used or reproduced in any manner whatsoever without
written permission except in the case of brief quotations
embodied in critical articles and reviews. Printed in
the United States of America. For information address
Harper & Row, Publishers, Inc. 10 East 53rd Street,
New York, N.Y. 10022. Published simultaneously in
Canada by Fitzhenry & Whiteside Limited, Toronto.
Designed by Harriett Barton
1 2 3 4 5 6 7 8 9 10
First Edition

1165

Library of Congress Cataloging in Publication Data
Chaikin, Miriam.
  Lower! Higher! You're a liar!

  "A Charlotte Zolotow book"—Half t.p.
  Summary: Ten-year-old Molly organizes a club to
boycott the neighborhood bully during a summer in
Brooklyn at the time of the second World War.
  [1. Jews—New York (N.Y.)—Fiction. 2. Bullies—
Fiction. 3. New York (N.Y.)—Fiction] I. Egielski,
Richard, ill. II. Title.
PZ7.C3487Lo   1984   [Fic]   83-48445
ISBN 0-06-021186-5
ISBN 0-06-021187-3 (lib. bdg.)

For the nieces and nephews:

Miriam, Sara, and Rebbecca Chaiken
(they spell it with an "e")
Michael and Steven Pearl,
and also Julie C.

Also by Miriam Chaikin

How Yossi Beat the Evil Urge

Getting Even

Finders Weepers

I Should Worry, I Should Care

Contents

1 Estelle's Tears   1

2 Five More Weeks   12

3 *Shabbos*   23

4 Boycott!   36

5 The Boycott Celia Club   45

6 The School Yard   55

7 Foiled Again!   64

8 Celia's New Friend   74

9 *Inner Sanctum*   85

10 Mrs. Chiodo Knows   97

11 The Bracelet   107

12 Estelle's Joy   114

13 An Ambulance Comes   121

14 Four More Weeks   129

LOWER!
HIGHER!
YOU'RE A
LIAR!

CHAPTER ONE

Estelle's Tears

Molly sat on the couch in the living room, reading. It was hot out, and all the windows were open. She brushed away the fly that landed on her book and turned the page. Except for the scraping sound that came from the kitchen—Mama was washing clothes on the washboard—the house was silent. Molly loved having the living room all to herself, and reading in peace and quiet.

Besides Mama, only Yaaki, Molly's baby brother, was at home. But he was in his crib, napping in the next room.

A mosquito came buzzing around Molly's nose and she swatted it away. She looked up suddenly, thinking she had heard Yaaki. Any unusual sound from her little brother worried her. He was beautiful and lively. But he had asthma. And sometimes, if he got upset, he had tantrums.

1

Everybody hurried to give him whatever he wanted, to keep him happy. He was worth it.

Molly put down her book and tiptoed into the next room to see if Yaaki was all right. He was sleeping peacefully. His blond curls were damp from the heat and lay flat against the pillow. Molly smiled, thinking that even asleep, he was beautiful. She tiptoed out and closed the door behind herself.

"Why don't you go outside and play?" Mama called from the kitchen.

"With who?" Molly said, joining her mother in the kitchen. She thought longingly of Tsippi, her best friend, who was away in the country for the summer.

"With whoever is outside," Mama said, scrubbing away.

"There's no one outside. I already looked."

"Look again," Mama said.

"That's what I hate about the summer," Molly said. "You can never find anybody to play with. Borough Park is dead in the summer."

"What about those girls who are here every day—Little Naomi, Lila, and that other girl, Shmilly?" Mama said.

Molly knew her mother was trying to be funny. "Ma, it's not Shmilly, and you know it. It's Lily." She thought about those girls. All together, they weren't worth one Tsippi. But they were better than nothing. "They're okay," she said.

2

Mama took the plug out of the sink and let the water run out. "There are plenty of other children too," she said. "I always see lots of children outside."

"Sure, little kids, like Rebecca," Molly said, speaking of her little sister. "Or older kids, Joey's age. But not my age." Sometimes, when Molly got started on something, she couldn't stop herself even when she wanted to. She had a feeling this was going to be one of those times.

"The girls my age are not around here. They go to Prospect Park. Or the Sunset Park pool. Or Coney Island," she said. "Their mothers take them everyplace," she added, knowing that wasn't true. She was ashamed of herself. She was just being mean. She knew her mother would have been glad to take her to the park or the pool, if she had the time. But Mama was afraid to travel around Brooklyn alone. She was born in Petah Tiqwa, a small town in Palestine. She never got used to the bigness of Brooklyn. That and the fact that her English wasn't good made her afraid to get on a trolley car or subway train. Papa was different. He learned English when he was in the army, during World War I. He knew how to travel everywhere.

Mama wiped her hands on a towel. "When you're twelve, you can go to Coney Island alone, with your friends," she said.

Molly stared at her mother. "Twelve!" she said. "I can't even get to be eleven. I've been ten and three-quarters for a million years. I'll never be twelve."

"You'll be, you'll see," Mama said in a singsong voice.

The hall door opened and Rebecca came in.

"Estelle's crying in the hall," she said, speaking to Molly.

Molly hardly knew Estelle. She wondered why the girl should be crying in her hall.

"What happened?" she asked.

Rebecca shrugged.

"Go see what's wrong, Molly," Mama said.

Molly and Rebecca ran out into the hall. Estelle stood facing the wall, leaning her head on her arm and crying.

"What happened?" Molly asked.

Estelle did not answer.

Molly saw that Estelle was really crying. "Did somebody hit you?" she asked, trying again.

Estelle shook her head.

"What then?"

"C-Celia," Estelle said between sobs.

"I should have known," Molly said. She had half guessed it. If anything rotten happened, Celia couldn't be too far away. Celia, her mother, and the boarder had lived in the neighborhood once before. Molly had thought, when they moved away, that she had seen the last of them. But a few weeks ago they had moved back, to the same build-

ing, the one next to Molly's, but to a different apartment. When Molly saw Celia on the stoop the first time, she couldn't believe her eyes.

"What did she do this time, that skunk?" Molly asked, glaring at the wall as if she could see right through it to Celia's hallway.

Estelle turned from the wall and faced Molly. Her eyes were red and watery. "I didn't want her to see me crying and call me crybaby. So I ran in here," she said, sniffling.

"But what did she do?" Molly asked again.

"I would—I wouldn't obey her," Estelle said with trembly lips.

"Sure," Molly said, knowing what Estelle meant and feeling wise. Any girl who became Celia's best friend had to become her slave. The girl had to do whatever Celia said. Molly never could understand any girl being so dumb as to become Celia's best friend.

"Well, what'd you expect?" Molly said. "If you were her best friend, you were her slave. You had to obey her."

Estelle began to cry all over again.

"Molly, make her stop," Rebecca said.

Molly had been so involved with Estelle, she had forgotten about Rebecca. "Go out and play—you're too young for this," she said.

"I am not," Rebecca said.

"I wanted a best friend," Estelle said, sobbing. "She said she would be it, if I obeyed her. At first it was easy. She's rich, and always has money to spend."

"Rich?" Molly said. She knew that was one of Celia's favorite lies. "A liar, that's what she is. There are no rich people living on this block."

Estelle sniffled, gazing at Molly with watery eyes.

"You want a hanky?" Rebecca asked.

Estelle shook her head. "She *is* rich, Molly," she said. "Her mother gives her two cents every day, just to buy candy. At first it was easy to obey her. Every time she bought a Hershey's or a twist she would say, 'You have to obey me. Take a bite.'"

"That doesn't sound like a slave to me," Rebecca said.

"*Shhh*, Rebecca. No one's talking to you," Molly said. "So what happened?" she asked Estelle. "She wouldn't give you a bite anymore?"

"No, nothing like that," Estelle said. "She took my bracelet. And I just bought it. In the five-and-ten. With my own money." She began to cry all over again.

Molly did not understand. "What do you mean, she took your bracelet?"

"She pulled it off my wrist and wouldn't give it back. . . ."

"Why?"

"Because—I wouldn't make faces at Florrie with her."

7

Molly was so mad, she could have spit. Celia always picked on people who couldn't fight back. It used to be Fat Anna, a woman who lived across the street who died. Now it was Florrie. Florrie also lived across the street, in one of the row houses. She might have been as old as fifteen, but she acted like a baby. She played with a handkerchief all day long. Or she stuck out her tongue, not at people, just to wet her lips. She smiled at odd times but she never bothered anybody. Molly liked Florrie a lot.

"*Oooo!* Is she rotten!" Molly said. "She's a real devil, torturing that poor thing."

"I didn't want to do it!" Estelle said quickly. "That's why she took my bracelet."

Molly wondered how Estelle's mother was going to react to the bracelet, if it was new. "Will your mother be mad at you for losing it?" she asked.

"I didn't lose it."

"You know what I mean."

Estelle shook her head. "She doesn't even know I have it. I bought it myself. She's always glued to the newspaper or radio, listening to the news." She dried her eyes with her hand. "She's worried about the war, and Hitler, you know. Her mother and father live in Poland."

Molly nodded. She understood. Her mother and father also worried about their relatives in Europe. Hitler, the head of Germany, was trying to conquer the world. In

every country he conquered, he killed all the Jews.

"I loved it s-s-sooo," Estelle said, crying.

"What are you going to do, Molly?" Rebecca asked.

Molly looked down at Rebecca. Rebecca was right. Something had to be done. What Celia had done was the same as stealing. She shouldn't be allowed to get away with it. It wasn't fair.

"I'll help you get your bracelet back," she said.

"How?" Estelle asked.

Molly realized she would have to think of something. In the meantime, she tried to appear determined.

"Where is she right now?" she said, trying to sound tough.

Estelle nodded at the door. "She was on her stoop when I ran in here. I don't know if she's still there."

"Let's go see," Molly said, opening the door and running out. She stood on the stoop, with Estelle and Rebecca behind her, and gazed across a little yard to the next stoop. Celia wasn't there. Secretly, Molly was relieved. Celia was the toughest girl on the block and Molly was afraid of her. But she acted brave and turned this way and that, searching the street for Celia.

The only people around were Joey, her brother, playing marbles against the curb with his friend Izzie, and Florrie, across the street. Molly waved to her, then turned back to Estelle.

"She's not here now. Either she's in her house, or she

went someplace. All we can do is wait," she said.

"I'm not waiting," Rebecca said.

"Who asked you to?" Molly said.

Rebecca gave Molly a sour look, took hold of the cement banister of the stoop, went slowly down the steps, and walked into the adjoining house.

"Where is she going?" Estelle asked.

Molly smiled. "Her best friend lives there. Mrs. Chiodo. Mrs. Chiodo is older than my mother," she added.

Molly saw Estelle's eyes open wide suddenly.

"There she is," Estelle said in a whisper.

Molly turned and saw Celia on her stoop. She was showing the bracelet on her wrist, and grinning.

"That's my bracelet," Estelle whispered.

"That's Estelle's bracelet!" Molly hollered across.

"Sez who?"

"Sez me!" Molly answered.

"Oh, yeah? Prove it!" Celia said. "This is my bracelet. It always was."

Molly looked at the little yard that separated her from Celia and figured it would take Celia a few seconds to come over, if she wanted to, and that Molly had enough time to run inside.

"Lower! Higher! She's a Liar!" she called, ready to open the door and run in if she saw Celia move.

Luck was with her. Celia's mother came out of the house.

The boarder who lived with them was with her. They said something to Celia; then all three of them walked down the steps of the stoop and went to the corner.

"What if she's going away forever?" Estelle asked.

"Don't be a jerk," Molly said. "Do you see satchels? Do you see valises? They'll be back," she said, turning to Estelle.

She saw Estelle's face puckering up and her lips becoming all trembly again.

"Don't worry, we'll get it back," she said, trying to comfort Estelle.

"I know. But how?" Estelle said.

Molly couldn't really say. She put up two fingers, in the V-for-victory sign that Churchill always used. "You'll see . . ." she said mysteriously.

CHAPTER TWO

Five More Weeks

The next day was Friday. And, as usual, Molly helped her mother get ready for *Shabbos.* That was the Jewish Sabbath. It started Friday night and ended Saturday night. And while Mama was busy cooking, Molly went about the house with a rag, dusting furniture.

She thought about Estelle as she worked. She still hadn't come up with any idea for getting the bracelet back. She told herself, as she put her dusting things away, that she would think of something in time.

Mama had spread the good silverware out on the table for her to polish. And Molly sat down at the table and began polishing. "I like polishing," she said to Mama, who was stirring a pot at the stove. "You have something to show for your work." She looked at her reflection in a knife.

"Look, Ma," she said, holding up the knife. "It shines like anything."

"Very nice," Mama said, carefully adding salt to a pot.

"Ma, you didn't even look," Molly said, annoyed. "I want a compliment."

"Who gives me compliments?" Mama said, making a face against the steam that rose from a pot she had uncovered.

Molly thought about that. It didn't seem true. "Everybody compliments you," she said. "On the *gefilte fish* . . ."

"The compliment is for the fish, not for me," Mama said.

Molly couldn't see the difference. But she wasn't interested enough to discuss the matter further. When she was

through, she took a pencil stub from the top of the refrigerator and opened the door of the broom closet. A calendar hung on the inside part of the door. With great relish, Molly crossed out the week that had just passed. She then counted the weeks remaining to Labor Day, in September.

"Five more weeks," she announced.

"And then what?" Mama asked.

"Then Tsippi comes home from the country. And school starts." School meant Molly's first term at Montauk Junior High. She hugged herself at the thought. "I can hardly wait."

"Only five weeks?" Mama said. "Where did the summer go? *Oy!* How time flies!"

Molly looked at her mother in surprise. "Flies? Ma, the summer is creeping like molasses. Each day is like a year."

"To you it creeps, to me it flies," Mama said. "When you get to be my age, it'll fly for you too."

Molly didn't want to insult her mother, but she couldn't see herself ever getting as old as Mama. She thought about the creeping part and wondered if Mama's idea of time had something to do with the fact that she was born in Palestine. "Ma," she said, "in America, time is the same for everybody. An hour is an hour, and a month is a month."

"What is it, the *mull-ess-iz?*" Mama asked.

"It's an expression for something slow. It's a syrup."

14

Molly was afraid to say more. Her family was kosher. She wasn't supposed to eat anything outside of her own home. She had tasted molasses once, at Tsippi's house, and Tsippi's stepmother wasn't kosher. Molly had only taken a taste. The molasses wasn't meat. It had *looked* kosher. "It comes out of the bottle slow, like ketchup," she said, to give Mama the idea.

Mama flung a white tablecloth over the table. "Take the other side, Molly," she said.

Molly laid the other side neatly down on the table and smoothed it. Rebecca and Yaaki came out of Joey's room, which was off the kitchen. Yaaki was carrying his basin. That was his chair. He took it wherever he went. When he wanted to sit, he put it on the floor and got in.

"You were so quiet in there," Molly said to them, "I didn't know you were home."

Yaaki went into the living room with his basin. And Rebecca kissed Ruthie, her little plastic doll with a dented belly, and laid her on the chair.

Molly watched the kitchen become transformed for *Shabbos* as Mama added candles to the table, and two *challa* breads. She covered the breads with an embroidered cloth.

"You want to invite the girl—what's-her-name—for *Shabbos*?" Mama asked.

Molly wondered who Mama was talking about. "What girl?"

15

"The one who was crying in the hall yesterday," Mama said.

Molly stared at her mother. "No, Ma, I don't want to invite her. I hardly know her."

"The Bible says you're supposed to invite people for *Shabbos*," Rebecca said.

Molly realized, as she looked at her sister, that Rebecca had pushed her into helping Estelle. Now she was trying to push her into inviting Estelle for *Shabbos*. "How do you know? You can't even read," Molly said. "Anyhow, I don't care what the Bible says."

Mama looked up. "Molly! What kind of thing is that to say?"

Molly hadn't meant what she said. She didn't know why she had said it. "The Bible doesn't say you have to invite somebody just because she was crying in your hall," she said, trying to get out of it.

"You're supposed to invite orphans and strangers," Rebecca said. "Papa told us."

Molly remembered that Estelle had spoken of a mother. She guessed she also had a father. "She has a mother and father, so she's not an orphan," she said.

"Then she could be a stranger," Rebecca said.

Molly was feeling trapped, and she didn't like it. "A stranger! You call somebody who goes to my school and who was crying in my hall a stranger?" she yelled.

Rebecca glared at her for a moment, then picked up Ruthie, her doll, and headed for Joey's room. Molly watched her go. There was something so sad looking about Rebecca walking away. Molly felt terrible. She was sorry she had yelled at her little sister.

"I'm going to the library," she called after her. "I'll get a book for you too."

With her helping work over, Molly went into the room she shared with Rebecca to get her library books. They were on her bureau, which stood between two windows. She tried not to look at the window on the right. It was special. She thought of it as God's window. She talked to God from there. As she turned to leave with the books, her eye accidentally fell on the right window. She had nothing important to say. But God might be looking. And she couldn't just ignore God. So she smiled up at the sky, giving a good, long smile, then went into the kitchen.

Mama was holding Yaaki up to the sink so he could drink from the faucet. He liked drinking water that way. Molly opened the front door to go out.

"Tell Joey I want to see him," Mama called after her.

Molly did not have far to go to find her brother. He was playing stoopball with Izzie when she went out.

"Mama wants you," she said, knowing Mama wanted him to help her get ready for *Shabbos*. But Molly said

no more, because Joey didn't want his friends to know he helped around the house.

Joey threw the ball to Izzie. "Catch!" he said. "It's your ball." He ran up the steps two at a time.

Molly walked on to the library. She always discussed what to take out with Mrs. Pearl, the librarian. And today, at the librarian's suggestion, she chose *David Copperfield* as her good book and *Nancy Drew and the Stolen Jade* as her other book. She always took two. The *Nancy Drew* was to read between chapters of the good book, to make the good book last longer. For Rebecca, Molly took out *Uncle Wiggily and His Friends.*

When she arrived home, she found everything ready for *Shabbos* and Joey walking around the table putting plates in front of each chair. There were six green plates and one white one. Aunt Bessie, Papa's sister, often came for *Shabbos.* She ate off the white plate. Mama got the green plates from the movies. Whenever it was dish night at the movies, Mama went to get a new plate.

Molly put her two books on the bureau and carried Rebecca's book into the kitchen.

Joey looked up. "Some girl—Estelle—was here," he said.

Molly felt funny. She had almost forgotten about Estelle. "Did she say anything?" she asked.

Joey shrugged. "She'll be back tomorrow, or the next day," he said.

That was fine with Molly. If Estelle wasn't in a hurry to get her bracelet back, neither was she. Also, she had more time to try and think of something.

"Hey, I have an idea," Joey said.

"What?" Molly asked, interested.

"I'm going to eat on the white plate tonight," he said. "Let Aunt Bessie have a green plate, with the rest of the family."

"Big deal!" Molly said. She loved her aunt. But Joey was Aunt Bessie's favorite. Everyone knew it. Molly often saw her aunt slipping Joey a nickel or a dime. Molly didn't really care. Joey wasn't anybody else's favorite, only Aunt Bessie's.

"Library time!" she called, taking the book into the living room, where Yaaki was sitting in his basin. He scrambled up.

Rebecca came running in. Molly seated herself on the couch and waited for Rebecca and Yaaki to settle themselves on either side of her.

"What did you get me?" Rebecca asked, looking at the book in Molly's lap.

Molly was pleased to see that Rebecca wasn't mad at her anymore. *"Uncle Wiggily and His Friends,"* she said.

"Uncle Wiggily is a gentleman rabbit," she added, repeating what Mrs. Pearl had told her.

"What's a rabbit?" Rebecca asked.

"A little white animal, smaller than a cat," Molly said.

She showed the picture in the book to Rebecca and Yaaki. The picture was of a rabbit standing on his hind legs and wearing knickers. "In real life, the rabbit can't stand," Molly said. "He doesn't wear pants either. He has four feet and he sort of hops."

She turned to the opening page. "The first story is called 'Uncle Wiggily and the Barber.'"

Rebecca nodded, her eye on the page.

" 'One day,' " Molly began, reading in her story-telling voice, " 'Uncle Wiggily Longears started out for a ride in his automobile. It had a turnip steering wheel—'"

"What's a turnip?" Rebecca asked.

Molly wasn't sure herself. She studied the picture looking for a clue, but found none. She read the rest of the sentence.

"It's something you eat," she said.

"Read. No talking," Yaaki said.

Molly continued. " 'It had a turnip steering wheel that he could nibble on when he was hungry.'"

"What's nibble?" Rebecca asked.

"Taking little bites," Molly said. She made small rapid movements with her lips, to show Rebecca what she meant. Then she read on, telling about Uncle Wiggily's adventures with his friends—a gentleman raccoon and a gentleman monkey.

"That's the end of the first story," she said, closing the book.

"How come the story is only about gentlemen?" Rebecca asked.

"It isn't," Molly said.

"You said Uncle Wiggily was a gentleman. Raccoon was a gentleman. Monkey was a gentleman. There are no lady gentlemen in the story."

"Ladies can't be gentlemen," Molly said. "Only men can be gentlemen. Anyhow," she added, "Jane Fuzzy Wuzzy is a lady. She's a muskrat who takes care of Uncle Wiggily. She's in the story too."

"But Uncle Wiggily goes out and has fun with his friends. Jane Fuzzy Wuzzy is like a mother. She doesn't have fun. She stays home and bakes pies for him. Is that why she isn't a gentleman?"

Molly didn't know what went on in the other stories. "Let's see. Maybe Jane Fuzzy Wuzzy has fun in the next story," she said.

Yaaki slid down from the couch, picked up his basin, and went into the kitchen.

"Should I read you another story?" Molly asked, still wanting to make it up to Rebecca for yelling.

Rebecca didn't have to think about it. The hall door opened and Papa and Aunt Bessie came in.

"Papa!" Rebecca cried, sliding from the couch and hurrying into the kitchen.

As Molly rose, she watched Papa pick Rebecca up in his arms, then Yaaki. She hated to admit it to herself,

but she was jealous. She knew it was silly. She was too big to be picked up. She had already started French. She put a smile on her face and went to join the others in the kitchen.

CHAPTER THREE

Shabbos

I n the kitchen, everyone stood laughing. When Molly saw Aunt Bessie, she joined in the laughter. Aunt Bessie stood still and stiff as a statue. She held her small *Shabbos* valise in one hand and a paper bag with the banana cake she always brought in the other. She looked funny, a fat lady standing there with eyes closed and making little breathing sounds through her nose. She was inhaling the smells of Mama's cooking.

"Even the angels won't have a better meal than us," Aunt Bessie said, opening her eyes.

Molly enjoyed her aunt's company, even if Joey was her aunt's favorite. Molly took the small valise from Aunt Bessie's hand and brought it into her room. That's where Aunt Bessie slept when she came, on a folding cot. Molly and Rebecca slept in the bed. Molly looked at the cot

and smiled. Even Aunt Bessie made jokes about somebody as fat as herself sleeping on a skinny cot. Molly returned to the kitchen.

"Six green plates, Laya," Aunt Bessie said to Mama, looking at the set table. "That means you didn't go to the movies this week."

Mama was dishing out portions of chopped liver onto individual small plates. "They weren't giving out big plates this week, so I didn't go," she said. "Next week they'll give out big plates."

"Anyhow," Molly said, "you have a green plate tonight. Tell her, Joey."

Aunt Bessie turned to look at Joey.

"I told them before," Joey said. "I'm eating on the white plate tonight. I want to."

Aunt Bessie beamed with delight. "Such a gentleman," she said. "Thank you, Joey."

"You see, Molly," Rebecca said. "If you do something, you're a gentleman. The one who cooks is the lady."

Molly pretended not to hear. There was no point in answering Rebecca. She could keep the same conversation going for hours, with her questions.

Papa came out of the bathroom, where he had gone to wash up, and put a *yarmulke*, a skull cap, on his head. He took a second one from the drawer and handed it to Joey. "Here, put it on," he said.

"Me too," Yaaki said.

Papa put one on Yaaki's head.

"Come, everybody. Sit down," Mama said.

Molly sat where she was, between Joey and Rebecca. Papa took his regular place, in front of the covered *challa* breads. He waited for Mama to settle Yaaki in the high chair. And when everyone was seated and quiet, he said the Hebrew words for the blessing over bread:

Blessed is God, Creator of the universe,
who causes food to grow in the earth.

Then he removed the embroidered cover, cut slices of one *challa*, sprinkled a dash of salt on each slice, and passed it down the table.

Molly took her slice, said her own blessing over the bread, and bit into it. She felt good. *Shabbos* was always special for her. It somehow pushed the war farther away and made her feel safer.

She could hear voices in the courtyard through the open kitchen window, sounds of other families having supper. Celia's window faced the courtyard too. Molly chased away the thought of her. She didn't want Celia in her head. She wanted to keep her peaceful feeling.

"Where's mine?" Rebecca asked.

"Coming," Papa said, giving Joey a slice to pass down to her.

"Did you have a busy week in the factory?" Mama asked Aunt Bessie.

"Don't ask," Aunt Bessie said. "I didn't have time even to breathe. But wait, wait. Next week I'll have plenty of time."

"Why?" Mama asked, looking up.

Molly knew Mama had a scare, wondering if Aunt Bessie had lost her job.

Aunt Bessie pinched off a piece of *challa* and popped it into her mouth. "We're going on strike. The foreman said we should be earning higher wages."

Molly could see Mama was relieved. "Good, good," Mama said. "It's nice to have a few extra pennies in the pay envelope."

Aunt Bessie smiled. "Only in America," she said. "You should see what they just invented. Silk stockings is finished, old-fashioned." She beamed. "The girl who sits at the machine next to me bought a new kind of stockings. It's the latest thing. Nylon, they call it. If I get a raise, I'll buy myself a pair."

She turned to Joey. "But if I don't win the strike, you'll have to support me, Joey," she said.

"Don't worry, I will," Joey answered without looking up from his plate.

"He should support you, with all those nickels and dimes you gave him," Molly thought.

"You know," Papa said, "*Shabbos* is not here yet, it's true. It starts when it gets dark. But even so, we should already begin to leave the regular week behind, and think of other things."

Molly knew what Papa meant. But she felt the smart-alecky side of herself creeping up on her. "Like what?" she asked.

"Like—the beautiful world that God created for us," Papa said.

"What's so beautiful about Hitler?" Molly said, regretting her words almost immediately.

Papa glared at her. "God made the world. Hitler's mother and father made Hitler," he said.

Molly wished she could stop doing things like that. Now she had made Papa angry. And on *Shabbos* too. She hurried to change the subject.

"Pa, you know the V-for-victory sign that Churchill always makes?" she said. She held up two fingers in example. "Where did that start? Did Churchill make it up?"

Papa wiped his mouth. He knew a lot and was always glad to answer questions. "I read somewhere that a radio announcer from Belgium started it," he said. "The word for victory starts with a V in his language. One day he made a V with his fingers, and it caught on."

"Victory starts with V in English too," Molly said, glad she had succeeded in changing the subject.

Papa nodded and went on eating.

"See how smart my brother is," Aunt Bessie said. "He got all the brains in the family. I was the dumb one."

Molly didn't like hearing that. "Don't say that," she said. "You're not dumb. Papa went to school longer than you, you told me yourself."

Everyone began speaking at once, telling Aunt Bessie that she wasn't dumb. As they did, Molly went around the table taking away the empty plates. Everyone *ooh*ed and *aah*ed as Mama brought the roast chicken to the table.

When Molly sat down again, she heard Celia's voice in the courtyard. She listened. Celia's mother said, "Quit pestering me. You get two cents every morning. That's more than any other kid gets."

Molly thought about what Estelle had told her. Then Estelle was right about the two cents. That still didn't change the fact that Celia was a big liar. Molly remembered the poem her father had once taught her:

> *This is the price liars have to pay:*
> *They are not believed when the truth they say.*

Everyone said how delicious the roast chicken and potatoes were. Molly was beginning to see what Mama had meant. They complimented the food, not the person who cooked it.

"How about complimenting Mama?" Molly said.

"What do you call what we're saying?" Joey said, gazing at the food on his plate.

Molly looked at Mama and shrugged. Mama smiled.

"Eat in health. Thank God we have food on the table," Mama said, and put a potato and a piece of chicken on Yaaki's plate.

Molly ate with pleasure, enjoying every bite, along with the rest of the family.

"We'll have dezoit when Papa comes home from *shul*," Mama said when everyone was through. *Shul* was the Jewish word for synagogue, where Papa went to pray, to welcome in the Sabbath.

Molly and Joey exchanged glances at Mama's pronunciation.

"Ma, not dezoit, de-*zurt*," Molly said.

"Never mind. I'm not going on the stage," Mama answered, helping Yaaki out of the high chair.

"Pa," Rebecca said, "I want to go to the synagod with you."

Molly and the others laughed. Rebecca thought, because people went there to pray, that the word was synagod.

"Of course," Papa said, getting up from the table. "Whoever wants to come is welcome."

"Me too," Yaaki said.

Papa nodded. "You want to come, Molly?" he asked.

Molly shook her head. Girls didn't have to go to the

synagogue. They could go only when they felt like it. She rarely felt like going on Friday nights. That was when she could have the living room almost to herself. She could hardly wait to start her new book in the peace and quiet.

"I want to read," she said.

"Fine," Papa said.

Papa, Joey, Rebecca, and Yaaki went to the synagogue. Mama and Aunt Bessie busied themselves in the kitchen.

Molly got her book and sat down on the couch. She loved this moment. Starting a new book was always special. She opened the book and ran the side of her hand over the first page. Then she flipped through it, to look at the pictures. Then, ready to begin, she turned to the page where the story started, and began to read. In moments she was lost in the life of David Copperfield, an orphan boy, in long-ago London. She heard Mama and Aunt Bessie say the prayer over the Sabbath candles in the kitchen, then read on, completely caught up in the events of the story. When Papa and the others came home, she stopped reading and went into the kitchen.

Molly took a seat at the table. "Where's Rebecca?" Mama asked.

"I went to pull down the shades in the living room," Rebecca said, returning. "You want the Germans to see us? They'll know we're Jewish when they see the candles. They'll kill us."

Papa took Rebecca in his arms. "Rebecca, there are no Germans in Borough Park," he said.

"There's nothing to worry about," Aunt Bessie said. "The American army is the best army in the world."

Molly added her two cents. "Rebecca, we're way over here in the kitchen. Nobody can see in here."

"But we're supposed to pull down the shades at night. Papa said so. He's an air warden," Rebecca said.

"She's right," Mama said, bringing a large bowl of stewed fruit to the table and dishing it out. "That's what we are supposed to do, since America went to war."

Rebecca looked at the table.

"I thought we were going to have dessert," she said.

"What do you call this?" Molly asked, taking a spoonful.

"Yeah—does this look like a yo-yo?" Joey said, eating.

"I want Aunt Bessie's banana cake," Rebecca said, sitting down.

"Oh, I was going to save it for tomorrow, for the company," Mama said. Molly's parents always had company on Saturday afternoons. "But all right—I'll get you a piece now."

Mama brought Rebecca and Yaaki each a piece of cake. And everyone sat around the table, eating and drinking and singing table hymns—short, lively songs that gave thanks to God for the blessings of health, food, and Sabbath rest. Papa and Aunt Bessie sang so-so. Mama and Joey

had really good voices. Rebecca and Yaaki mostly made sounds. Molly sang the loudest. She had a rotten voice. In school she was a listener, and was made to sit in silence in back of the room. But at home, nobody stopped her from singing, and she sang at the top of her voice, ignoring the pained looks on Joey's face.

The next morning Molly did go to *shul* with Papa. She spent most of the time outside, playing and talking with other kids. When the services were over, she and her family went home for the *Shabbos* afternoon meal and more table songs. After lunch she left everyone sitting in the kitchen and went into the living room to read. After a while, company came. Soon it became too noisy for Molly to read as Mama and Papa and their friends drank tea in the kitchen and talked worriedly about the war.

As Molly put down her book, she saw the hall door open and Little Naomi, Lily, and Lila come in. She was not surprised to see them. They knew there was always candy in Molly's house on Saturdays and they often dropped in.

The girls smiled at the grown-ups around the table and walked through the kitchen.

Molly waved them in.

"Hi," they said, entering the living room.

Little Naomi was very tall. She was called Little because

she was shorter than another girl in school, Big Naomi. She sat down in the green chair, Papa's chair, under the picture of Jabotinsky, the Jewish leader. Lily and Lila joined Molly on the couch.

Molly looked forward to their reaction to her news. "Guess what," she said.

"What?" they asked eagerly.

She told them all that had happened and about her promise to help Estelle get her bracelet back.

"Can you beat that?" Lily said, looking from one girl to the other. "It's the same as stealing, taking something. . . ." They all shook their heads in disbelief.

Mama came in with a dish of candies, put it on the table in front of the couch, and returned to the kitchen.

"Thanks," Molly's friends called after her. Lily and Lila reached into the dish for a candy. Little Naomi had to get up for one.

"So what are you going to do to get the bracelet back?" Little Naomi asked.

"Yeah, what?" Lily asked, chewing away on a caramel.

Molly's anger at Celia was strengthened by the reaction of the girls. "We can't let her get away with something like that," she said. "Hitler started the same way."

"It's for justice," Little Naomi said. "We'll help you. Won't we?" she asked, looking around.

"Do you have any ideas?" Lila asked, studying the candy dish before choosing a candy.

Molly wished she had. "I'm still thinking," she said importantly.

CHAPTER FOUR

Boycott!

Papa and Joey went to the synagogue for the end-of-Sabbath services. Rebecca and Yaaki sat around the kitchen table helping Mama pull the green leaves from the tops of strawberries. Molly sat curled up in the frame of the kitchen window, listening to the sounds of people talking in the courtyard. She thought it odd that Estelle hadn't bothered to appear. She reviewed the conversation she had had with the girls. They were all agreed that something had to be done about Celia. But what, she wondered. What would make a person like Celia give the bracelet back?

Aunt Bessie came into the kitchen with her little valise. She had packed her things, and was ready to leave after supper.

"Don't fall out," she said to Molly.

"I won't," Molly answered.

In a while Papa and Joey came home.

"A good week!" they called as they entered.

Molly got down from the window. "A good week," she answered with the others. Then she went to stand with the rest of her family for the end-of-Sabbath ceremony, as Rebecca held the candle and Papa said the blessing.

"Let's eat," Joey said, sitting down at the table. Molly sat next to him. Mama topped each bowl of strawberries with a glob of sour cream and gave it to Joey to pass down the table.

"Well, Monday starts the fun," Aunt Bessie said.

Molly knew she was talking about the strike. She had an idea suddenly. There was something like a strike, but different. She had once heard her aunt telling about it.

"Aunt Bessie," she said, "what is the other thing that workers do when they're not satisfied? When they want to complain about something?"

"What other thing?" Aunt Bessie asked.

"When they stop working, they go on strike, right?"

"Right."

"There's another thing. I heard you talk about it," Molly said. "The workers tell people not to shop in a certain store. Or not to buy something."

"You mean a boycott?" Papa asked.

"That's it, a boycott!" Molly said.

Mama added sour cream to another bowl and gave it to Joey to pass.

"A boycott is a powerful thing," Papa said. "You can boycott not only a store or a factory, but a country too. Take the war in Europe. Even before America went to war, many Americans refused to buy German goods. They boycotted goods made in Germany."

Molly became elated. She felt she had hit on something. Celia wasn't afraid of a thing. Nothing could scare her. But maybe a boycott could make her give the bracelet back. She had no friends, with Estelle gone. She would start to get lonely soon. Maybe, if everybody stopped talking to her, she might become miserable enough to change.

"I have to help somebody get something back and I need everyone's help," she said.

Papa looked up. "It sounds mysterious. Who is the somebody? Why do you have to do it? And what is the something?"

"A girl from school," Molly said.

"She was crying in the hall," Rebecca added. She examined the bowl Joey had passed her. "I'm not supposed to get this," she said, pushing the bowl away.

Mama clapped a hand to her face in surprise. "Woe is me," she said, getting up. "I forgot you don't like strawber-

ries." She sliced a banana into an empty bowl, added sour cream, and gave it to Rebecca.

"Well?" Molly said, looking around the table.

"Well what?" Papa said. "You told us who, but you didn't tell us what happened."

"Celia made Estelle cry," Molly said.

"What'd she do, hit her?" Joey asked.

"That's all you can think of, hit," Molly said. "People cry for other reasons too."

"No hitting," Yaaki said, taking the spoon away from Mama and feeding himself.

"Nobody's hitting," Mama said.

"I still don't understand the problem," Papa said.

Molly sighed with annoyance and started all over again. She spoke slowly, enunciating each word. "Celia, the girl next door, took away this girl Estelle's bracelet. And won't give it back," she said.

"That doesn't sound right," Papa said.

"It isn't, Pa. It's not fair," Molly said.

"Celia? That nice little girl?" Mama asked.

Molly looked at her mother in disbelief. "Nice? Ma! How can you say that? She's mean. A liar. A crook. And she curses cripples."

Mama looked away. "Then she's not so nice."

"Oh, girls!" Joey said.

"And boys are angels, I suppose," Molly said.

39

"No, but they don't do things like that."

"No, they just fight and get bloody noses," Molly said.

"Enough!" Papa said.

"Children," Mama said, "how many times do I have to tell you? I don't want arguments, or bad words, at the table. It's not nice behavior. And it's not good for the digestion."

"I didn't say any bad words, Mama," Rebecca said.

"Me too," Yaaki said.

"No, you are wonderful children," Mama said.

"And I suppose I'm not?" Molly said.

"Who said no?" Mama said. "Of course you are. You all are," she added, glancing around the table at each one. "Why are you making such a force?"

Molly and Joey looked at each other and laughed.

"What's so funny?" Mama asked.

"Not force, Ma. *Fuss*," Molly said.

"It sounds the same to me," Mama said.

"So tell us about your friend Celia," Papa said.

"Friend! She's my enemy," Molly said.

"I mean the other girl—"

"Estelle," Rebecca said.

"Estelle," Papa repeated. He turned to Molly. "What do you want us to do?"

"Celia did something illegal," Molly said. "I want everyone in this room to boycott her." She looked around the

table. "If she talks to you, don't answer. If she looks at you, don't look back."

"I live in Coney Island, not around here. But I'll be glad to boycott her," Aunt Bessie said.

"I never talk to her," Mama said. "Sometimes I say good morning, if I see her with her mother."

Molly saw that she had not succeeded in getting across the idea of how rotten Celia really was. "Ma," she said, "she's a very bad person. She could grow up to be another Hitler."

"*Oy!* That's bad," Mama said. "I won't even say good morning. I'll boycott."

"Do you still say boycott if it's a girl?" Rebecca asked.

Molly laughed with the others.

"It's still boycott," Joey said.

"I'll boycott her too," Rebecca said.

"She hangs around watching us play ball sometimes," Joey said, scooping up the last sour cream in the bowl with a piece of bread. "But I never talk to her."

"But will you boycott her?" Molly asked.

"Sure," Joey said. He got up and put his empty plate in the sink.

"Bring in the radio, Joey," Papa said. "The news will be on soon."

"Am I going to hear music?" Yaaki asked.

"After the news," Mama said. "Cake Smith will be on."

"Ma!" Molly and Joey called together.

"What?" Mama asked, facing them.

Molly looked at Joey and smiled. "Ma," she said. "We told you a hundred times. *Kate* Smith. Not Cake."

Mama got up and started clearing the table. "It's hard to remember everything—" she said.

"So what do you say?" Molly asked. "Can I count on this family to boycott Celia?"

"I will," Rebecca said again.

"Me too," Yaaki said.

Joey brought in the radio from the living room, put it on the kitchen table, and plugged it in.

"What about you, Pa?" Molly asked. "Will you boycott her?"

Papa glanced at the clock on the refrigerator, to be sure not to miss the news. "I will, if you show me who she is," he said. "But first I want to hear Gabriel Heatter."

"Pa, I'm not kidding," Molly said.

"Neither am I," Papa said.

"Whose turn is it to dry?" Joey asked.

Molly was always happy when it was her brother's turn to help with the dishes. "Yours," she sang out.

Aunt Bessie got up and went to the sink. "I'll tell you what," she said. "Joey was such a gentleman, giving me the green plate, I'll take his turn for him."

Joey's face lit up. "Thanks. My friends are waiting for me," he said, and ran to the door.

"She not only gives him money but does the dishes for him too," Molly thought. But she felt too good to let it bother her. She had been dying of boredom all summer long. Now, at last, something was happening. What's more, she had the support of her whole family.

"I have the best family in the world," she said.

"No you don't," Mama said from the sink. "I do."

"Ma!" Molly said, half annoyed and half amused.

"Shhh," Papa said, turning on the radio. Something was wrong with the radio and no sound would come up unless someone held the loose wire in back. He fixed his chair so he could rest his hand on the table, and took hold of the wire.

The voice of Gabriel Heatter, the news announcer, filled the room.

"There's bad news tonight," he said.

Molly and the others sat forward to listen.

"A report has come in from Czestochowa, a town in Poland, that thousands of half-naked Jewish men and women were beaten until they bled. Young girls were taken into the synagogue by the guards, where they were raped and tortured."

Molly's heart lurched with fright.

Papa's lips were white with anger.

"Woe is me!" Mama said.

"Guttenu! God!" Aunt Bessie said softly.

Molly felt a pounding in her ears. The war news was

often terrible. The news about the Jews was always awful. The Nazis were killing and torturing them. Why were people always picking on the Jews? What had the Jews ever done to them? Molly wondered how God could let such things happen. She knew she wasn't being loyal to God, thinking such a thought, but she couldn't help it.

Gabriel Heatter said that the Germans had bombed London again. He gave more war news. Then he began to tell the news of America. President Roosevelt had made a speech to the farmers. Molly didn't care about that. Her thoughts returned to Celia and the boycott.

CHAPTER FIVE

The Boycott Celia Club

The next morning Molly was so excited at breakfast, she could hardly sit still. The idea of a boycott had grown. It had turned into the idea for a club. She even had a name for it, the Boycott Celia Club—B.C.C. for short. She couldn't wait to tell the girls.

After breakfast, she took her rubber-band ball, and a package of rubber bands, and went outside. Her idea was to sit on the stoop and look for members for the club. Her house was between Thirteenth and Fourteenth avenues. Everyone went to Thirteenth Avenue to shop. That's where all the stores and pushcarts were. Sooner or later, everyone passed her house on the way there.

She made herself comfortable, with her back against the wall and her legs stretched out in front of her. She put the rubber bands in her lap and began adding them

to the ball. The ball was still very small. She hoped she had enough rubber bands to make a difference. The store-keeper had told her these were the last rubber bands in the store. He wouldn't have any more to sell until after the war. Rubber bands had become scarce. So had lots of other things. Soldiers and sailors came first. Everything —cloth for uniforms, food, rubber bands—went to them. It was only fair.

As she worked on the ball, she watched the street. A few girls went by, but they were either too old or too young. When she had added the last rubber band, Molly looked at the ball. It was quite a good size now. She bounced it and was pleased to see how high it went.

"Hey, Molly!" a voice called.

She turned and saw Little Naomi skating down the street. Little Naomi was not a good skater. She moved as if her feet were stuck in tar. Molly could hardly wait to tell her the news.

"Whew!" Little Naomi said, grabbing hold of Molly's stoop to bring herself to a stop. "Did you think of anything for us to do about getting Estelle's bracelet back?" she asked.

"You bet," Molly replied readily. "Did you ever hear of a boycott?"

"Sure. What is it?"

Molly explained. "That's what we're going to do," she

said. "And I even have a name for the club—Boycott Celia Club. B.C.C. for short," she added proudly.

Little Naomi let go of the stoop and started rolling away, then caught herself again. "She's crazy," she said. "I wouldn't talk to her if she were the last person on earth."

Molly was disappointed. She had thought Little Naomi would be jumping for joy at the idea of a club. "Well, that makes you a member," she said, testing Little Naomi.

"Who else belongs?" Little Naomi asked.

Molly realized that Little Naomi didn't want to be a part of anything until she was sure the other girls were members too.

"Who? Only my whole family, including my brother Joey," Molly said. "Plus me, and you—and Estelle—and Lily and Lila," she added, trying to make it sound like as many people as possible. "If Tsippi were here, she'd belong too."

"Okay, I'll join," Little Naomi said. She glanced down at some coins in her hand. "I better go," she said. "My mother is waiting for her roll. She just dies if she doesn't have a roll and butter with her coffee for breakfast." She skated away. "See you later," she called.

"Tell Big Naomi," Molly called after her. "Maybe she wants to join too."

"She went to the country with her mother this morning, for two weeks," Little Naomi answered without looking back.

Molly was pleased to have her first real member, someone who wasn't in the family. She watched the passersby. One girl her age passed, but she was stuck up and never talked to anyone. She was glad to see Lily and Lila coming down the street and motioned to them to hurry.

"Listen to this," Molly said, as they came running up the steps of the stoop. They listened wide-eyed as she told them all about the club. "Little Naomi was just here. She's a member too," she said.

Lila frowned. "When you boycott cereal, you don't buy it," Lila said. "But how do you boycott a person?"

"You ignore them," Molly said, "make believe you never saw them. You do it a million times a day in school."

"I'll join," Lily said.

"I will too," Lila said.

"Great!" Molly said, thrilled.

Lila rumpled up her face. "Wait a minute," she said. "Is that all we have to do, ignore her?"

Molly nodded.

"But I never see her. How is she going to know I'm ignoring her?" Lila said.

"A club makes a program. That's what it's for," Molly said. She thought a moment. "She's in the school yard a lot. We'll go there after lunch and see if she's there."

"And then what?" Lila asked.

"We'll boycott her! What do you think?" Molly said.

"Ignore her, right?" Lily said.

"Right," Molly answered.

"Okay by me," Lila said.

"But look," Molly said. "Don't go into the school yard. We'll meet outside, and go in together."

"In front of the girls' entrance, or the boys'?" Lila asked.

"The girls'," Molly said. That entrance was on her side of the street.

"Okay," Lila said.

"If I see anybody else, should I bring her?" Lily said.

"Sure," Molly said. She remembered Little Naomi. Little Naomi would have to be told. "Lily," she said, "you live near Little Naomi. Tell her where to meet us."

Lily nodded.

"Come on," Lila said, pulling Lily by the arm. "I have to get to Thirteenth Avenue. My mother is waiting for the onions."

"I'll tell her," Lily called, allowing herself to be pulled away.

It occurred to Molly, as she watched them go, that she had gotten a club together all for Estelle. And that Estelle was the only one who knew nothing of the plan. Molly didn't know where Estelle lived, or she would have gone to call on her. She shrugged. If Estelle didn't show up in time, she thought, they could always have the boycott without her.

Florrie came out across the street, and Molly crossed

over to talk to her. Molly used the same soft voice for
Florrie as she used for her baby brother.

"Hi, Florrie," she said.

Florrie sat twisting her handkerchief. She smiled.

"Did I ever show you my rubber-band ball?" Molly
asked, holding it up.

Florrie nodded.

"I made it," Molly said.

"Yeah?" Florrie asked.

"It's easy," Molly said. "You just keep putting rubber
bands over a marble, or something hard, until you have
a ball." She bounced it a couple of times. "See how high
it goes?"

Florrie watched the ball rise and fall.

The rhythm of the bouncing ball caught Molly up too,
and she began to recite, turning her leg over the ball as
it bounced her way,

> *"One, two, three a nation,*
> *doctor, doctor, there's a patient*
> *waiting for an operation,*
> *one, two, three a nation."*

"Molly!" Molly recognized Mama's voice and turned
to look across the street. Mama was leaning out of the
window.

"Rebecca's coming out—keep an eye on her," Mama
said.

Molly was annoyed. She did not feel like watching Rebecca. But Mama disappeared from the window before she could protest. In the next moment, the stoop door opened and Rebecca came out. She stood on the stoop looking across at Molly.

"Come here, if you want to," Molly called. She was curious about whether Rebecca would obey the rules for crossing, and waited to see what her sister did. Rebecca obeyed all the rules, looking both ways to see that no cars were coming, then hurrying across.

Rebecca came up to Molly and took her hand. Molly saw Rebecca force herself to smile. Rebecca liked Florrie. But she didn't understand her differentness.

"Hi, Florrie," Rebecca said between tight lips.

Florrie gave a sudden twist to the handkerchief and smiled.

"Do you want to try the ball, Florrie?" Molly asked.

Florrie shook her head.

"Go ahead, try," Molly said, holding the ball up to her.

"I can't," Florrie said.

"All you have to do is drop the ball," Molly said. "It comes back by itself. Watch." She dropped the ball and let it bounce back.

Florrie's mother came to the window. "Florrie, come in for lunch," she said.

Florrie got up. She put her hand in her pocket and took

out two chicken-feed candies and gave Molly and Rebecca each one.

"Thanks," the girls said, taking the candy.

Florrie went inside, and Molly and Rebecca crossed over to their side of the street. When they got there, Rebecca held the candy up to Molly.

"You take it—I don't want it," she said.

"Why?" Molly asked.

"Her finger was on it."

"So what?"

"She might be catching," Rebecca said.

Molly popped both candies into her mouth.

"Here comes Estelle," Rebecca said, and ran over to play with Shimmy, a little boy who lived down the street.

Molly felt a surge of excitement.

Estelle waved and came running.

"Hi," Estelle said, all smiles.

Molly was glad to see Estelle, for reasons of the club. But she hoped Estelle wasn't going to think they were going to be best friends.

"I have good news," Molly said, sounding official.

"You got the bracelet back!" Estelle said.

Molly stared back. "Are you kidding?" she said. "What do I look like, Mrs. Roosevelt or somebody?"

"What then?" Estelle asked, shifting her weight from one foot to the other.

Molly wondered if it was a habit or if Estelle had to

go to the bathroom. She told Estelle about the boycott and the club idea that grew out of it.

Estelle's face clouded over and she stopped shifting and stood still. Instead of praise, Molly got a look of disappointment.

"What's the matter?" she asked.

Estelle was silent a moment. "I'm afraid of her, Molly," she said. "She might kill me."

Molly knew that Celia was mean. But she didn't see her killing anyone.

"She can't kill you—it's against the law," she said.

"But what if she kills me first, then the cops come?"

"Look," Molly said. "There are five of us in the club. We'll be together all the time. She can't harm you." Molly was afraid of Celia herself. But not the way Estelle was. "I live here, right next door to her, and I'm not afraid," she said.

Her words had the right effect. Estelle's face softened.

"I won't have to do anything alone?" she asked.

"We'll do everything together," Molly said. "That's what a club is for."

"Gee, Molly," Estelle said, "the club was a great idea. Who thought of it?"

"Who do you think?" Molly asked. She was pleased with herself inside. But she said nothing more so as not to brag.

CHAPTER SIX

The School Yard

For lunch, Mama put out tuna-fish sandwiches. Joey had already finished. He had gobbled his down and run out again, still chewing. Molly, Rebecca, Yaaki, and Mama were at the table, eating. Yaaki sang aloud to himself. And Molly was busy imagining the excitement that lay in store for her that afternoon.

She felt a twinge of guilt suddenly. She had written Tsippi that she missed her every second. But she had thought of Tsippi only twice that day. To make up for it, she tried to think only of Tsippi during lunch. It didn't work. She couldn't picture Tsippi in the country, because she didn't know what the country looked like. She had heard the country was full of trees and looked like a park. But instead of Tsippi, all she could see in her mind's eye was the trolley car she had once taken to get to Prospect Park.

She drank down her glass of milk and went to the sink to wash her plate. She noticed that Rebecca was through eating.

"Give me your plate, and I'll wash it," she said.

"I'm still eating," Rebecca said, munching on a green olive.

"You don't need a plate for an olive," Molly said.

"I need it for the pit," Rebecca said.

Mama went into the other room to get the ironing.

As Molly did the dishes, Mama set up the ironing board in the kitchen. Molly began to hurry. Rebecca caught on to things fast. If Rebecca knew Molly was going to the school yard, she'd want to come along too.

"Little Naomi's uncle is an air-raid warden, like Papa," Molly said, trying to introduce a new subject.

"You going to get the bracelet?" Rebecca asked.

"What?" Molly asked, as if she hadn't heard. Rebecca gave her the creeps sometimes.

"Estelle's bracelet. Are you going to get it back today?"

Molly did not answer. That was the best way to deal with Rebecca. She dried the dishes with a fury, as if she were too busy to think of anything else.

" 'Fane, Molly," Yaaki said.

She knew what he meant and went into her room to get it. Everyone always hurried to give Yaaki what he wanted. He liked the sound that paper made when it

opened out after being crumpled. She kept a supply in
her drawer, just for him. What he was asking for today
was a new kind of paper. It had just been invented.
It was invisible, and you could see through it. Cellophane
was its name.

She returned with a piece and gave it to him.

"What do you say?" she asked.

"Fanks," he said, pinching the cellophane between his
fingers, then holding it up to his ear to listen to the sound
it made coming apart.

"I'm going," Molly said, heading for the front door.

"I'm finished eating," Rebecca said, sliding off her chair
and looking at Molly.

Molly pretended she hadn't heard. She hurried out and
ran up the street and across Fourteenth Avenue to the
school. P.S. 164 took up the whole front of the block,
from Forty-second to Forty-third streets. Behind it was the
school yard, surrounded by a high wire fence. Molly crept
up to where the school ended and the yard began. From
there, she could see into the school yard without being
seen. Peering through the fence, she saw Joey and some
boys playing ring-a-levio. A few girls were playing double
Dutch rope.

She gave a start. There was Celia, standing beside Mrs.
Rice, the gym teacher, watching a bean-bag race. Molly
wished the other girls would hurry. As she looked up,

she saw Little Naomi, Lily, and Lila. She motioned to them to come quickly and at the same time put a finger to her lips, telling them not to speak.

"There she is," Molly whispered, pointing inside.

The girls peered through the fence.

"Is she the one playing double Dutch?" Lily asked.

Molly stared at her. "You mean you don't know who Celia is?"

"I thought I did," Lily said.

"She's the one standing next to Mrs. Rice, watching the race," Molly said.

Lily peered inside. "Oh, that's her? I know her too," she said.

"Okay, so what do we do now?" Little Naomi asked.

"Hey, Molly!" Estelle called from the corner, and came running.

Molly walked with the girls to the open gate, the girls' entrance.

"This is what we'll do," she said, as everyone gathered around her.

"Everybody hold arms, like this," she said, hooking her arm with Little Naomi's. "We'll walk into the school yard together. And the minute she sees us, turn your heads!"

Lila giggled. "You think she'll get the hint?"

"She'll get it, all right," Molly said. "She's bad, but not dumb." She linked arms with Lily on the other side. All the girls stood with arms linked.

"Stay close, and look straight ahead," Molly said.

Huddled close to each other, shoulder to shoulder, arms linked, Molly and the other girls marched into the school yard. Molly glanced over at Estelle, to see if she looked afraid. Her face was whitish but her feet were moving.

"Hey, what are you supposed to be doing?" one of the girls playing double Dutch asked.

"Don't answer," Molly said. "Keep walking."

She marched on with the girls, toward the race. Celia stood facing them. She would have seen them, but she never looked up. Her eyes were on the runners.

"Walk a little slower. Give her a chance to see us," Molly said.

"She's not looking," Little Naomi whispered.

"I know," Molly whispered back.

"We'll be on the boys' side in a minute, if we keep walking," Lily whispered.

"When we get to the race, stop," Molly said. "We'll just stand there. Stare at her. And the minute she looks, turn your head."

"Left or right?" Lily asked.

Molly didn't think it mattered. "Right," she said, just to give an answer.

She and the girls arrived at the race and stopped. They stood with arms linked, staring at Celia and waiting to be noticed. But Celia never glanced their way.

"Who wants to run against the winner?" Mrs. Rice asked.

"Me!" Celia said.

"Now she'll never notice us," Little Naomi whispered.

"Shhh," Molly said.

Mrs. Rice blew the whistle and Celia ran. She won. She won the next race too.

"Is everyone too tired? Or should we go for a ten-yard dash?" Mrs. Rice asked.

The girls standing around her started jumping up and down. "Yeah, yeah," they said, wanting to run.

"Come this way," Mrs. Rice said, and led them to another part of the school yard.

Molly and her friends were left standing, arms linked and alone.

"Should we go too?" Little Naomi asked.

"No," Molly said, releasing her arms. Everyone dropped arms.

"Whew, what a relief," Lily said, batting her eyes. "My eyeballs were killing me."

Little Naomi and Lily also fluttered their eyelids, to show their eyes were tired too.

"What do we do now?" Little Naomi asked.

"Try again tomorrow?" Lily asked.

Molly wasn't sure. She was disappointed. "Maybe we should try something else tomorrow," she said. "Let's meet

at my house after lunch. We'll have a meeting and discuss it."

"Okey-dokey," Lily said.

"I'm going out the boys' entrance," Little Naomi said. "I'm going to my uncle's. He's on that side."

"I'll go with you," Lily said.

"Me too," Lila said.

They ran across the school yard, and Molly and Estelle walked out the way they had come in.

"Molly," Estelle said, "I really appreciate your helping me."

Estelle's words cheered Molly up. "You have to stop bad people," she said. "That's the way Hitler started. Nobody stopped him."

The girls parted at the corner, Estelle turning to go up Fourteenth Avenue and Molly crossing the avenue to go home. Now that she was alone, she felt really blue. She hated to fail.

Mama was still ironing in the kitchen when Molly went in. She plunked herself down on a chair without a hello.

"Has the cat got your pajamas?" Mama asked.

"You didn't say it right," Molly said.

"So what's the right way?" Mama asked.

Molly couldn't remember. And didn't want to be bothered thinking about it. "You made me forget," she said.

Mama looked up. "I made you forget?"

Molly laughed at herself for being so silly. She got up and gave Mama a hug. "I'm just upset because the boycott didn't work," she said.

Mama finished the handkerchief and put it on the finished pile.

"Didn't you tell me yourself," Mama said, "if you don't succeed, try again and again."

"Yeah . . ." Molly said, not bothering to correct her mother. "Oh—I remembered the other thing," she said. "One is *Has the cat got your tongue?* And the other is *the cat's pajamas.* You got them mixed up."

"It's crazy. Who wouldn't get it mixed up?" Mama said. She nodded at the finished pile. "Molly, take the things and put them away, please."

Molly went with the things from room to room, putting them in the right drawers. Yaaki was asleep in her room, so she tiptoed in. He woke as she slid open the drawer. She was sorry to disturb his rest. "Shhh, go back to sleep," she said softly.

Yaaki stood up in the crib. "I'm finished. Take me out," he said, opening his arms.

She lifted him out and carried him into the kitchen. She hoped Mama wasn't going to be angry at her for waking him. Yaaki needed his rest.

"He got up," Molly said apologetically.

Mama glanced at the clock on the refrigerator. "He

slept enough," she said. "Give him a bottle milk."

"No. Glass!" Yaaki said.

Molly sat him in his high chair and poured a glass of milk for him. She sat down in the chair next to him. "I'll hold the glass for you," she said.

"No!" he said, and took the glass in both hands.

Molly kept her hand ready under the glass, just in case.

"What do you think I should do to make Celia give back the bracelet, Yaaki?" she asked her brother playfully.

"Tell her mama," Yaaki said between gulps.

"Maybe he's right," Mama said, taking up Papa's shirt to iron it.

Molly realized, as she thought about it, that she was as afraid of Celia's mother as she was of Celia. Celia's mother was tough too. "Naaa," she said.

She sat slumped in her chair, one hand under Yaaki's glass, wishing she had something nice to think about. She remembered it was Sunday. That was when the best radio programs were on. Eddie Cantor, Red Skelton, *Major Bowes and His Original Amateur Hour*, Charlie McCarthy. Then there was her book, *David Copperfield.* She had two good things to think about.

She felt much better suddenly.

CHAPTER SEVEN

Foiled Again!

Molly sat on the stoop, waiting for the girls to appear. She had thought and thought all morning. And at last she had come up with a boycott idea. Now that she had, she was eager to see them.

Before long, Little Naomi, Lily, Lila, and Estelle came running from the corner. Molly decided to test them, to see if any of them had gone to the trouble to think.

"I Ii," she said, answering their greeting. "Does anybody have any boycott ideas?"

The girls looked at each other as if they were hearing about a boycott for the first time. Molly thought as much.

"Well, I do," she said, trying not to sound too pleased with herself.

"What is it? Tell us," they said.

"I have the whole thing all figured out," Molly said. The girls were all ears.

"We tried the school yard, and it didn't work," she continued. "I don't know where she is when she's not in the school yard. But I do know one thing: She's always in the same place before suppertime."

"Where?" Little Naomi asked.

Molly nodded across the little yard. "Right there, on her stoop. She's always there, waiting for her mother to come home from work."

"Then that's when we should do something," Lily said.

"Let Molly finish," Estelle said.

The attention she was receiving pleased Molly. She reminded herself of Nancy Drew. "We can't wait on my stoop—we don't want her to see us," she said. "We have to wait someplace else."

"Where?" Lila asked, looking around. "I don't see any good hiding places."

Molly nodded toward the corner, on the other side of the street. "The candy store," she said.

"Mr. Rubel!" Little Naomi said, looking toward the store. "He hates children. He doesn't even let you walk into the store until you show him your money."

Molly held up a penny. "I went shopping for my mother this morning. There was a penny change, and she let me keep it."

"I have two cents," Little Naomi said.

"I have a penny," Lila said, feeling in her pocket.

"Me, too," Lily said. ". . . I was going to save it."

Estelle looked down at the ground. "I spent all my allowance, till the end of the month, on the bracelet," she said. "It cost forty-nine cents."

"Maybe Little Naomi can lend you a penny," Molly said. She saw Little Naomi squirm and make a face. "I know what," she added. "I'll have another penny soon. Lend me the penny, Naomi, and I'll lend mine to Estelle."

"I'll give it back as soon as I get one," Estelle said.

The pennies were exchanged.

"There," Molly said. "Now we all have money. Now we can all go into the store, and Mr. Rubel won't stop us. We'll wait inside, so we can watch the stoop. Then, when we see her, we'll run out."

Little Naomi nodded with approval.

"Sounds like a good idea to me," Lily said.

"Yeah—but you said her mother comes home before supper," Lila said. "We just finished lunch. We can't go into the store now. Mr. Rubel won't let us stay there so long."

"I didn't mean now, silly," Molly said. "I meant later."

"Well, what are we going to do now?" Lily asked.

Molly shrugged. She didn't care.

"I know," Lila said. "Let's go to Ocean Parkway and watch the rich kids ride their bicycles."

"Let's go to the chicken market and watch the man pluck chickens," Estelle said.

Molly did not want to do that. "Pugh!" she said, holding her nose. "It stinks there."

"Then let's go to the bakery, for the good smells," Lily said.

"There's too many of us," Molly said. "They'll never let us in."

"Why don't we just take a walk on Thirteenth Avenue?" Little Naomi said.

"That's the best idea," Molly said.

She and the girls went down from the stoop and walked to Thirteenth Avenue. They strolled along between the rows of pushcarts on the gutter side and the stores on the other side, looking at everything. Lots of people were out shopping, and the avenue was crowded.

Molly stopped in front of the tailor shop. "Let's see if Julie is home," she said. She made a megaphone of her hands and called up.

"Julie!"

A moment later Julie appeared in the window. She blew her curly hair out of her eyes as she smiled down at Molly.

"We're going for a walk—want to come?" Molly asked.

Julie looked downcast. "I better not," she said. "My mother doesn't feel too hot. I better stay home."

Molly whispered out of the side of her mouth, so only the girls could hear, "Her mother makes believe she's sick. She gets Julie to stay home that way."

She shouted up to Julie. "Too bad," she said. She suddenly felt that she had been disloyal to Julie. She was sorry. "Come over sometime, okay?" she said.

Julie was always pleased to be invited. "I will," she said, nodding her head vigorously.

Molly waved good-bye, and she and the other girls walked on. When they reached the end of the row of pushcarts, they crossed over and walked back on the other side. That side of the street was even more crowded, and Molly and the others kept having to separate, to let people pass.

"Molly!" Little Naomi said suddenly. "There she is!"

"Where?" Molly asked, trying to peer between the man and woman in front of her. She couldn't see much, but Little Naomi, being tall, could.

"Near the sour pickle lady," Little Naomi said.

"Hurry," Molly said. "Link arms."

Quickly the girls got into the boycott position. Shoulder to shoulder they moved down the crowded street. The people around were annoyed.

"Listen! Who do you think you are?" one woman said, shoving herself through.

"You don't own the sidewalk!" another woman said, knocking Molly's arm from Estelle's.

Molly quickly fitted her arm back into Estelle's. "Is she still there?" she asked Little Naomi.

"No," Little Naomi said, standing on her toes and looking over the heads. "She's by the delicatessen now."

Molly and the girls tried to walk in the boycott position but couldn't. It was impossible. There were too many people on the street. And everyone was annoyed and looking daggers at them.

Frustrated, Molly dropped Estelle's arm. "Oh, let's skip it," she said. "We'll do it later, like we said."

It was hot walking in the sun, and Molly and the girls went into the five-and-ten to cool off. It wasn't really cool there, but it was shady. They walked between the counters looking around.

"My bracelet!" Estelle cried suddenly.

Molly looked where Estelle was pointing and saw a gold bracelet, with little gold hearts suspended from it. She took Estelle by the arm to comfort her.

"Come on, let's leave," she said, thinking that was the best way to spare Estelle's feelings.

They went out. Cartons were strewn about in front of the baby furniture store next door. The awning over the store was open, casting shade below. Molly saw a sign in the window and went up to read it: *Closed due to a death in the family.*

She turned to the girls with a smile. "Lucky us," she said. "We can sit in the shade."

She climbed up on one carton and the other girls found

seats of their own. They sat talking—about school, dentists, and girls who were boy crazy.

"Hey, do you think we should go to the boycott?" Lila asked after a while.

Molly agreed that the time had come. They got down from their seats and headed for Molly's block.

"Let's walk on the candy store side of the street," Molly said. "That way, we'll see her before she sees us. If she's there, we'll go into the candy store one by one. She won't notice us then."

When the girls saw that Celia's stoop was empty, they hurried up the street. Florrie was sitting outside and Molly waved to her.

"What's wrong with her?" Estelle whispered across to Molly.

"She's really sweet," Molly said. "It's a sickness. But it's not catching," she added, remembering Rebecca's fear.

"They call people like that morons," Lily said.

"I wondered," Estelle said. "There's one living in my aunt's building, too."

"It's incurable," Little Naomi said.

"She's so sweet. I like her," Molly said, and came to a stop a few feet from the candy store.

"Let's get out our money," she said, holding up her penny.

The girls all took out their money

"I'll buy something," Molly said. "I'll watch the stoop from the window, but you take your time, till she comes. Act like you can't make up your minds."

Molly opened the door. "Show him your money right away," she whispered.

The girls went in holding up their coins. Mr. Rubel was leaning on a counter, reading the paper. He looked up, saw that they all had money, and went back to reading.

Molly bought a candy banana, because she could make it last long. She stood looking out the window, nibbling and watching Celia's stoop. The girls were busy looking over the candy section and trying to make up their minds.

Molly saw Celia come out of her house. "There she is!" she said. "Hurry, choose."

The girls quickly made their choices and handed over their pennies. They shoved the candies into their mouths, all except Estelle. She had chosen a rope of licorice. It would take her forever to eat it. Molly and the girls stood staring at her.

"I love licorice!" she said. "What should I do?"

"Stick it in your blouse," Molly said.

"Ugh! And then she's going to eat it?" Little Naomi said.

"Come on," Molly said. "Hurry!"

Estelle shoved the licorice down her blouse, and went out with the others. Outside, Molly and the other girls linked arms and hurried across the street in the boycott

position. Celia stood on her stoop, facing them.

"When we get close, turn your head and look the other way," Molly said.

Celia outwitted them. As the girls drew near, she turned around, slow and easy, and stood with her back to them. The girls found themselves looking at the back of her head.

"Never mind, keep walking," Molly said out of the side of her mouth. "Let's not give her the satisfaction."

As if they were walking that way just for the fun of it, they passed Celia's house and arrived at the steps of Molly's house. Molly knew, if she turned around, she would now find Celia facing the other way. But she didn't look.

"Walk up my stoop this way," she said. "Little Naomi will open the door for us."

Arms linked, they went up each step together, then, as Little Naomi opened the door, turned sideways to go inside. Once in Molly's hall, they dropped arms.

"Boy! Can you beat her!" Little Naomi said.

"Skunk!" Molly said, angry.

"Skunk is right!" Lily said.

Estelle took the licorice from her blouse. "Anybody want a bite?" she asked, holding it up.

"Ugh!" Little Naomi said.

"Why?" Estelle said. "I'm wearing an undershirt. . . ."

Molly tore off a hunk and put it in her mouth. "Don't worry, we'll get her yet," she said, biting down hard.

CHAPTER EIGHT

Celia's New Friend

As Molly sat at the breakfast table with Mama and Yaaki, the hall door opened and Estelle came flying in. Molly was surprised. Estelle had never been in her house before. She seemed quite at home, barging in.

"Hello, hello, hello," Estelle said, glancing around the table and giving each one a separate greeting. She stared at Yaaki.

"Look at those blond curls," she said. "What a beautiful baby."

"I can walk. I'm not a baby," Yaaki said.

Molly wondered what had brought Estelle.

"First, here's the penny I owe you," Estelle said. "I helped the lady upstairs with her groceries, and she gave me a penny."

"Is that all?" Molly said, wondering.

"No," Estelle said. "You'll never guess."

Molly waited to hear more but Estelle was silent. "What?" she asked finally.

"She has a new best friend!" Estelle said.

Molly couldn't believe her ears. Estelle could only be talking about one person. "Celia?" she asked.

"Yep," Estelle said, nodding.

"How do you know?"

"I just saw them! In the school yard! The two of them were walking together, holding arms."

Molly found it hard to accept. "Are you sure?"

Mama got up and took the empty cups from the table.

"I told you. I just saw them!" Estelle repeated.

"Who is the girl?" Molly asked.

Estelle shrugged. "I don't know her name. She goes to our school."

Molly was disturbed by the news. But she was more curious than anything else and had to go out and see for herself.

"Let's go to the school yard," she said, jumping up from the table and running to the door.

"Don't get lost," Mama called after her.

"I'm just going to the school yard," Molly answered, and ran out. She was on the stoop before she realized that Estelle wasn't behind her. She opened the hall door and Estelle came slowly out.

"What's the matter with you?" Molly asked.

"I'm afraid to go back there. I think she saw me. If

she sees me again, she'll think I'm spying on her."

Molly was annoyed with Estelle. "We had two boycotts. She didn't do anything to you."

"Yeah—but there were five of us. Now there's only you and me."

Molly was afraid of Celia too. But she didn't think any harm would come to her from just looking. "Are you coming or not?" she said, heading for the corner.

Estelle fell in beside her.

"Anyhow, she won't see us," Molly said. "We'll hide behind the building and look through the fence."

Rebecca was playing with Shimmy in front of his house, and Molly stopped to speak to her. She wanted to be sure her little sister would be all right.

"I'm going to the school yard for a minute with Estelle," she said. "What are you not allowed to do?"

"Cross the street alone," Rebecca said.

"And what else?"

"Talk to strangers."

"And . . . ?"

Rebecca thought for a moment. "And take anything from strangers."

"Or else . . . ?"

"Or else I might get kidnapped, like the Lindbergh baby."

The answer satisfied Molly. She turned to Estelle. "Come on," she said, hurrying on to the corner.

They crept along the side of the school building, Molly in front and Estelle behind her. At the fence, Molly kept herself hidden behind the building and craned her neck to look into the school yard. Her eyes went from group to group until she spotted Celia. She was sitting in a doorway with another girl.

"She's there, all right," she whispered.

"Is the girl still with her?" Estelle asked, keeping behind Molly.

Molly nodded. "I can't see who it is. Her back is to me." She leaned forward for a better look. "They're eating something. Candy, I think."

Estelle crept forward for a quick look, then hurried to her place behind Molly again. "Sure," she said, "that's how she gets friends. With candy." She tapped Molly on the shoulder. "You're wrong there, Molly," she said. "Celia *is* rich. She was in my class when I had Miss Theiss. I heard her tell Miss Theiss. She wouldn't lie to the teacher."

Molly had never had Miss Theiss. But she knew all the kids liked her. Even Celia valued Miss Theiss' opinion. But that wouldn't keep her from lying.

"Oh, no?" Molly said. "A liar will lie to anybody, even her own mother." She turned to Estelle. "She once told me she had a brother. That was a lie. She can't even tell the truth about what she had for breakfast." Molly shook her head. "Everything she says is a lie—except maybe for

the two cents," she added, remembering the conversation she had overheard in the courtyard.

Estelle glanced over Molly's shoulder. "*Ooo!* They're getting up," she said, moving out of sight again.

Molly turned to look. She stared at what she saw. "I can't believe this," she said.

"What?" Estelle asked.

"It's Beverly," Molly said.

"Who's Beverly?"

Molly turned to face Estelle. "A girl in my class. She sat next to me. She's as big a liar as Celia, and just as rotten."

"Birds of a feather . . ." Estelle said. "Ohhh," she added in a cranky voice. "Now I'll never be able to get my bracelet back."

"Why not?" Molly asked.

"She only has one friend at a time. She'll never notice that we're boycotting her. She won't care. She has a friend. That's all she needs."

Molly had to admit to herself that Estelle was right. If Celia had one friend, she didn't care about anything else. The boycott was not going to work now. Disappointed, she started for the corner.

Estelle ran after her. "Are you mad at me?"

"Why should I be?" Molly said. She wasn't really mad at Estelle. She just wanted to be alone. She was tired and

disgusted. She had tried everything she could think of, and failed.

"I just have to get home," she said. "My little sister is alone. You saw. I'm supposed to be minding her."

"Can I come with you?"

"No, because then I have to help my mother," Molly said, making up an excuse.

They walked to the corner in silence. As Molly was about to part from Estelle, she remembered that she was baby-sitting tonight. Papa had a meeting of the Jewish War Veterans. And Mama was going to the movies. It was dish night. Molly didn't like to baby-sit alone. Once in a while Joey stayed with her, but she couldn't count on him.

"I have to baby-sit tonight," she said. "You want to come over and sit with me? We can listen to the radio. Baby Snooks is on."

Estelle shifted from foot to foot again. Molly still didn't know if that was a habit or what.

"I have to ask my mother," Estelle said.

Annoyed, Molly started to cross over. She didn't know why she couldn't get a straight yes or no answer.

"Maybe I'll see you before that," Estelle called. "Aren't the girls coming to your house? For the club . . . ?"

Molly thought they probably were. They would be expecting to take part in another boycott. She had no more

boycott or any other ideas for them. Her brains were all used up. She didn't feel like seeing them.

"Do me a favor," she said.

"Sure."

"You know where Little Naomi lives?"

Estelle nodded.

"Tell her the club is not doing anything this afternoon because I have to help my mother. Tell her to come tomorrow. And tell her to tell the other girls too."

Estelle seemed glad to have something to do. "Sure," she said, skipping off.

Molly crossed over and walked home. Rebecca was still playing with Shimmy. "I'm here," she said, as she went by.

Rebecca looked up. "Mama said there's a letter for you."

Molly's heart leaped with excitement. The letter had to be from Tsippi! "Why didn't you tell me before?" she said.

"There was no before. I just saw you," Rebecca said, and turned back to Shimmy.

Molly ran up the steps and into the house. Mama was sitting at the kitchen table, shelling peas, and throwing the empty pods into her lap. Yaaki was in his basin, on the floor, singing to himself. Molly couldn't resist giving him a kiss.

He wiped his cheek on his shoulder. "Don't," he said, and went back to his song.

"Where's my letter?" Molly asked.

"It's a postcard. On the refrigerator," Mama said.

Molly took the card and held it lovingly. She sat down at the table to read it. The card was mostly all about the weather. It rained a lot in Monticello and Tsippi was stuck in the bungalow with her stepmother most of the time. And there were hardly any girls, or even boys, her age up there.

Molly was glad Tsippi wasn't having a good time. Maybe she would bother her stepmother to bring her home before Labor Day. She pressed the card to her heart.

"I'm so lucky to have a best friend like Tsippi," she said.

Shoving peas from the pod with a finger, Mama said, "You said the same thing about your other best friends—Selma, Faigl, Norma . . ."

Molly didn't think she had felt as strongly about the other girls and was about to protest. Then she remembered how much they had meant to her—before they had moved away, or she had moved away, or something else had parted them.

"You know, Ma," she said, "sometimes I can't remember what they looked like."

"That happens," Mama said, getting up and holding the hem of her dress to toss the pods into the garbage pail.

"So how is the boycott going?" she asked, sitting down

again. "Maybe I should say girlcott, for Rebecca's sake."

"Not so good," Molly said, sorry to be reminded.

"Why?"

"You heard Estelle. Celia has a new best friend. She'll never notice that we're boycotting her. She only needs one friend at a time," Molly said.

"She's some fast worker," Mama said.

"I'll say." Molly wondered how someone as disgusting as Celia could find a friend so quickly, even if it was only Beverly.

Yaaki started to sing at the top of his voice, and Mama and Molly turned to look at him.

"I don't know what to do now," Molly said. "If Tsippi were here, she'd help me think. But these girls, they just come ready to do something. They never have any ideas."

"Maybe you should make friends with Celia's new friend and get her to join the boycott club too," Mama said.

Molly thought about that for a moment. "She's too disgusting," she said. "It's not worth it." *Birds of a feather,* she thought, remembering Estelle's phrase.

"That Celia is such a liar," she said. "She tells everyone she's rich, even the teacher." She glanced out the kitchen window. "Would she live here if she were rich? She doesn't even have a telephone! And the boarder! Would her mother take in a boarder if they were rich?"

"Some boarder!" Mama said out of the side of her mouth.

Molly wondered why people always sounded so funny when the boarder was mentioned. It wasn't only Mama. All the mothers in the neighborhood sounded the same way. There was something fishy about the boarder.

"Molly," Mama said, "I need eggs and bread."

Molly did not feel like running an errand. "Why do I always have to go?"

Mama looked around the kitchen. Only Yaaki was there. "Yaaki, would you go for me?" she asked.

Yaaki laughed.

"Why can't Joey go?" Molly asked.

"Do you see Joey here?"

Molly knew she was acting silly. "He's never home. I have to do everything," she said. "He gets away with murder."

"You have something important to do?" Mama asked.

"I was going to answer Tsippi's letter."

"If I have no eggs, I can't make supper," Mama said. "I have an idea," she added.

Molly looked up.

"It's your turn to dry the dishes tonight," Mama said. "I'll tell him to dry, because you went shopping. You can write your letter after supper."

Molly felt appeased. She took the card into her room

and put it in her drawer, under the paper lining, where no one would see it.

Mama handed her two quarters. "Buy some candy for tonight, too," she said. "And keep the change."

Molly went to the door.

"Go to the nice egg man, not the one I don't talk to," Mama called after her.

Outside, Molly saw Mrs. Chiodo getting into a car and waved to her. Molly waved to the driver, too. It was John, Mrs. Chiodo's married son. He was taking her for a ride.

As Molly walked to the corner, she had an idea. She and her family had been living on the block only a couple of years. But Mrs. Chiodo had been living in the same house for years. She probably knew what was fishy about Celia's boarder.

Glad to have a new thought in her head, Molly hurried off to the nice egg man.

CHAPTER NINE

Inner Sanctum

As Mama had promised, Molly did not have to do the dishes. Mama washed, and Joey dried. And Molly sat at the kitchen table, answering Tsippi's letter. So far she had written:

Dear Tsippi,

I am writing you a letter although you only sent me a postcard. I guess I miss you more than you miss me. I am not being sarcastic. It is just a joke. *Ha-ha.*

Molly wrote on, telling Tsippi about Estelle and the bracelet. She mentioned the boycott but did not go into details. It would have made the letter too long. She wrote other news, about who was away for the summer, and who was back, adding *ha-ha*s after whatever she thought

was funny. Some *Ha-Ha*s she wrote with capital H's and others with small h's, because she wasn't sure which was right. She finished by saying:

> I hope the summer gets over soon, so you can be back. We miss you—your favorite neighborhood, Borough Park, and your best friend (I hope still), me.

The *me* didn't look right, so she crossed it out and wrote *I.* That didn't look right either, so she crossed that out too, changed the comma to a period, and wrote *Love, Molly.*

She carefully copied Tsippi's Monticello address onto an envelope. Rebecca stood at her side, watching.

"Does everybody learn how to write?" Rebecca asked.

"Sure," Molly said.

"Everybody in the world?"

"If they want to."

"It looks hard."

"It is hard, but everybody learns. Even the dumb kids," Molly added, licking the envelope to seal it.

Rebecca turned to Mama, at the sink. "Ma, Molly said I was dumb," she said.

Molly glared at her little sister. "I did not!"

"She didn't, Rebecca," Mama said, handing Joey a dish to dry. "I heard what she said."

"I said *even* dumb kids," Molly said. "Wash out your ears next time."

"You don't have to answer her so fresh," Mama said. "She's only a child."

Molly stared at her sister. "Some child!"

"You said 'even,'" Rebecca said, pouting. "Who's even?"

"Kids who are left back," Molly said.

Rebecca stood staring.

"Kids who get left back twice," Molly said, staring back. She knew she was laying it on thick, but Rebecca had asked for it. "Some kids get left back again and again and never get out of the fifth grade," she added for good measure.

"Are all kids in the fifth grade dumb?" Rebecca asked.

Molly got up. "Yes," she said into Rebecca's face. She turned to Mama. "Ma, I need a three-cent stamp."

"On the bureau, under the derly," Mama said, turning off the tap.

Molly looked at her mother. "Ma, not derly. *Doily.*"

Mama lifted Yaaki and sat him on the table, to tie his shoelace. "Didn't you tell me not to say oily?" she said.

Molly and Joey looked at each other and smiled. It was hard to get Mama to understand the differences between sounds.

"That's right," Molly said. "It's *early*, not oily."

Mama put Yaaki down and gave Molly an exasperated look. "The English language is too hard for me," she said.

She turned to Joey. "You'll finish alone?" she asked.

"Yeah," Joey said, wiping a dish and putting it away.

Papa came into the kitchen. He was all dressed up to go to his meeting. Molly got the stamp and put it on her envelope. "Pa," she said, handing him the letter, "mail this for me when you go out."

Papa put the envelope in his shirt pocket. "Isn't anybody going to tell me how I look?" he said.

"You look nice, Papa," Molly and the other children called out.

"Thank you," Papa said, smoothing down his shirt collar.

"Give my regards to the old soldiers at the post," Joey called as Papa went to the door.

Papa made a V-for-victory sign with his fingers and went out.

Mama glanced at the clock. "I better get ready too," she said. "Mrs. Baumfeld is going to the movies with me. She'll be down any minute." She took off her apron.

"What dish are they giving out tonight, Ma?" Molly asked.

"The big green one," Mama said.

"Goody," Molly said. "Now Aunt Bessie won't feel like an orphan anymore. She'll have a green plate too, like the rest of us."

"What's playing, Ma?" Joey asked.

"The two singers," Mama answered. "The blond boy, and the pretty girl."

Molly turned to Joey. "She means Jeanette MacDonald and Nelson Eddy," she said.

Mama went into the bedroom to comb her hair and put on lipstick. She returned with her pocketbook. In the same moment, the hall door opened and Mrs. Baumfeld came in.

"Hello, children," she said, looking around. "*Nu*, you're ready?" she asked Mama.

Mama nodded.

Molly whispered in Joey's ear, "Let's tell Mama she looks nice," she said.

"Ma," Molly and Joey said together, "you look very nice."

Mama looked pleased. "A little lipstick," she said. She turned to Rebecca and Yaaki, seated at the table.

"Children, when I'm not here, Molly is boss," she said. "When she says something, you have to listen."

"Hey, why is she boss?" Joey asked. "I'm older!"

"You're older, but she's the one who stays home to watch the children. You run out with your friends," Mama said.

Molly felt important.

"Bye-bye," Mama called, leaving with Mrs. Baumfeld.

Joey put away the last dish and closed the cupboard door. "What program are you going to listen to tonight?" he asked Molly.

"Baby Snooks," Molly said.

"I want to hear *The Singing Lady*," Rebecca said.

"She's not on tonight," Molly said.

"I want 'Bistu Shane,'" Yaaki said. Molly knew he meant *"Bei Mir Bist Du Schön,"* a song the Andrews Sisters sang.

"They're not on tonight either," she said.

"Tell you what," Joey said, drying his hands on his pants. "I'll make a deal with you. I'll stay home tonight if you listen to my program."

Molly would have given anything to have his company. She hated sitting by herself. She had asked Estelle to come over, but Estelle was so vague, Molly couldn't count on her.

"What's your program?" she asked, trying not to sound eager.

Joey twirled an imaginary mustache. *"Inner Sanctum,"* he said in a creepy voice.

Molly knew that program. It was scary. She wasn't sure how the kids would take it. Yaaki was all right. He was too young to understand the program, and just sat to keep them company. But Rebecca might get scared. Molly spoke pig Latin to Joey, so Rebecca wouldn't understand.

"on't-Way ebecca-Ray et-gay ared-scay?" (Won't Rebecca get scared?)

"Naa," Joey said. "I'm home."

Molly turned to Rebecca and Yaaki. "We'll listen to *Inner Sanctum*, okay?"

They ran into the living room to get ready, Yaaki carrying his basin.

"I'll be right in with the candy," Molly said. She thought of Florrie as she poured the chicken feed candy she had bought into a dish. As she turned away, she noticed that she had left the change, three pennies, on the cupboard counter. Mama had said she could keep them. The two charity boxes that were kept on the counter seemed to stare back at her. She dropped a penny into each box and held one out for herself, hoping God was looking and certain that God would think that was fair.

"Candy!" she said, bringing the dish into the living room. Yaaki and Rebecca sat in the center of the living-room floor, Yaaki in his basin, and Rebecca on the floor next to him.

Joey perched himself on the arm of the couch so he could reach the wire in back of the radio, to hold it. He turned on the sound. The theme music of the program that had just ended came on.

Molly took a handful of candies, dropped a few into Joey's hand, and seated herself in Papa's green chair, under the picture of Jabotinsky. She sat facing Joey.

Silence followed the music.

"Here it comes," she said, feeling a little creepy already.

The sound of a squeaky, rusty door being opened was heard. Molly shuddered. She could just see the evil hand that was on the door, opening it.

The announcer, speaking in a slow, spooky voice, said:

Good evening, friends. This is your host, Raymond, inviting you through the gory portals of the squeaking door. I hope you have a friend with you tonight. If so, stay close, huddle together. Because a fiend *is loose in the streets tonight.*

The program hadn't even started and Molly was scared already. She put a smile on her face as she glanced at Yaaki and Rebecca.

The announcer laughed in an evil way: *"Heh-heh-heh."*

Molly could feel her heart knocking against her chest. In the next moment she was seized by a real fright. She had heard footsteps, not on the radio but in the house, real footsteps, drawing ever closer. She stared at Joey, too scared to speak. Joey had heard them too. He also looked scared. Molly felt faint. She grasped the arms of the chair and stared down at the floor, trying to hold herself together. A pair of shoes, a girl's shoes, appeared before her eyes. Molly looked up slowly.

"What's going on here?" Estelle said.

Molly was still too much in the grip of terror to speak.

"You scared Molly and Joey," Rebecca said.

"Scared me??" Joey said. "Are you kidding?"

Molly forced her voice out. "She—" Her voice shook

and she swallowed to clear it. "She did not," she said.

She realized what had happened. Rebecca and Yaaki could see Estelle enter the house. She and Joey couldn't. They could only hear footsteps. Molly pretended not to know that Joey had looked scared too.

The voice on the radio droned on.

Molly spoke pig Latin to Joey.

"et's-Lay urn-tay it-ay off-ay. e-Thay ids-kay are-ay ared-scay," she said. (Let's turn it off. The kids are scared.)

"Huh?" Estelle said, scratching her head.

Molly could see that Estelle did not understand pig Latin.

Joey turned the radio off.

Molly was still a little shaky. She wanted to change the mood in the house. "Let's sing," she said.

Estelle took some candies from the dish on the floor and went to sit on the couch.

"Sing, Joey," Yaaki said.

Molly thought that was a good idea. "Joey will entertain us," she said, in a radio announcer voice. "He is the best singer in Brooklyn."

"Cut it out," Joey said, looking embarrassed and sliding off the arm, onto the couch.

"Who's that, your grandfather?" Estelle asked, nodding at the picture over Molly's head.

"No, that's Jabotinsky, a Jewish leader," Molly said.

"Sing 'Bistu Shane,'" Yaaki said.

"I want my song," Rebecca said.

Molly turned to her little sister. "What's your song?"

"The Singing Lady," Rebecca said.

"I told you, she's not on tonight," Molly said.

"Say the song for me," Rebecca said.

Molly knew what Rebecca meant. *The Singing Lady* always opened her program with the same words. Rebecca called it a song. Molly repeated the words.

> *"Children, you who wish to hear*
> *songs and stories, come, draw near;*
> *both young and old come, hand in hand,*
> *and we'll be off to storyland."*

Rebecca smiled at Molly as if she had received a present. "Storyland," she repeated with a pleased look on her face.

Molly looked at Estelle, sitting next to Joey. Life was funny. Last week Molly had hardly known Estelle. Now she was sitting in the living room. And Molly was breaking her head, trying to get Estelle's bracelet back. Molly reminded herself to talk to Mrs. Chiodo tomorrow.

"Joey, do you know 'This Is Worth Fighting For'?" Estelle asked.

Joey nodded.

"Come on, Joey, sing," Estelle said.

Joey smiled and shook his head.

"He has a really good voice," Molly said. "Everybody

in the building comes to the window to listen when he sings.''

"Naa, they don't,'' Joey said, looking embarrassed.

"They do, Joey—they tell me,'' Molly said.

"Okay,'' Joey said. He cleared his throat. "My first song is *'Bei Mir Bist Du Schön,'* for Yaaki.''

He glanced at Yaaki and began to sing.

CHAPTER TEN

Mrs. Chiodo Knows

The next morning, Molly stood in front of the mirror combing her hair and thinking about Mrs. Chiodo. Mrs. Chiodo had to know what was fishy about Celia's boarder. Maybe it was something that could help Molly get Estelle's bracelet back. It was worth a try.

Molly remembered, as she put down the comb, that she had been meaning to see how she looked with a side part. Bette Davis was her favorite actress. She had worn a side part in her last movie, and Molly had been wanting to try it out. She parted her hair at the side, but it would not lie flat. It stood up. She spit on her hand and wet her hair, but it didn't help. Molly wondered why Bette Davis had no trouble keeping her hair flat. She returned to her center part and went into the kitchen.

Mama and Yaaki were eating breakfast. The green plate

97

that Mama had brought home from the movies last night was still on the table.

Mama looked at Molly as she sat down. "You got scared last night?" Mama asked.

Molly was annoyed with Rebecca for noticing, and for telling.

"Who said so? As if I didn't know," she said.

"A little boidy," Mama answered.

Molly buttered her roll and didn't bother to correct Mama.

"Rebecca told," Yaaki said, his mouth red with the jelly from the doughnut.

"I knew who it was," Molly said. "You didn't have to tell me." She glanced at Mama. "She's only a little kid. What does she know? I didn't get scared. Why should I? It was only a radio program."

As she ate, Molly thought about the girls. They would be coming around in a while, wanting to do something.

Molly was sure Estelle would have told them about Celia's new friend. They wouldn't expect to do another boycott, but they would want to do something.

Molly washed the dishes that she found in the sink and ran to the door.

"Don't go far. It looks like rain," Mama called after her.

Outside, Molly saw Rebecca playing with Shimmy.

"Rebecca!" she called from the stoop.

Rebecca looked up.

"Come here a minute," Molly said.

"I'm busy."

"It'll only take a second."

Rebecca came over.

"I need you to do me a favor," Molly said.

"What?" Rebecca asked suspiciously.

"Take me into Mrs. Chiodo's house. I have to talk to her."

"Why can't you go yourself?" Rebecca asked.

"She's your friend," Molly said. "Besides, I was never in her house before." She saw Rebecca weakening. "Come on," she said. "It'll only take a second. Just walk in with me. Then you can go back to Shimmy."

Rebecca marched silently into Mrs. Chiodo's entryway and went up the steps. Molly hurried after her.

Mrs. Chiodo seemed surprised to see them.

"Rebecca! Molly!" she said.

"I didn't come for myself," Rebecca said. "I just brought my sister. She wants to talk to you. I have to go."

"Shoo," Mrs. Chiodo said, motioning Molly in.

As Mrs. Chiodo went to close the door behind Rebecca, Molly stood in the kitchen sniffing in the aroma. The smells of cooking filled the room. Italian cooking smelled a lot different from Jewish cooking.

"What can I do for you, Molly?" Mrs. Chiodo asked with a smile.

"It's about Celia," Molly said. "The girl next door?"

Mrs. Chiodo made a sorrowful face. *"Sì,"* she said.

"She took a girl's bracelet—" Molly began.

Mrs. Chiodo put a hand to her cheek in surprise. "She stole it?"

"Not exactly," Molly said. "She—just took it. . . . Off the girl's hand. And she won't give it back."

"Poor thing," Mrs. Chiodo said. "What can you expect? The mother goes to work. The father in jail."

Molly was shocked. "In jail?" she repeated. Celia had told her that her father was dead.

"Sì," Mrs. Chiodo said. "He did something when Celia was small—I don't know what. Something bad," she added.

Molly felt woozy and understood for the first time the meaning of the expression *You could have knocked me over*

with a feather. She was sure the slightest touch could knock her down.

"But nobody talks about it," Mrs. Chiodo said. "What for?"

She went to the cupboard and took down a round tin. As she opened it, the most wonderful smell wafted out. "Cookies," she said, holding the tin up to Molly. "Take one."

The cookies were all different shapes. Molly wasn't allowed to eat anything that wasn't kosher. She would never touch meat, because it might be pork. But the cookies looked kosher to her. The round ones were biggest. She chose a round one and bit into it. "Umm, delicious."

Mrs. Chiodo smiled. She brought out a long, skinny cookie from the tin. "Give this to Rebecca," she said. "She likes this kind."

Molly thanked Mrs. Chiodo and went out. She handed Rebecca the cookie, then went to sit on the stoop, where she could think. She had lots to think about. She saw, as she glanced about, that Mama was right. The sky was growing dark. It *was* going to rain.

Across the street, Florrie came out. Molly watched her. Florrie took out her handkerchief as she sat down. She opened it and began twisting it, staring at it, as if she were playing an interesting game.

As Molly glanced away, she saw Celia and Beverly walk-

ing toward Florrie's house. Molly leaped up. Those two had no business walking on that side of the street, unless they were up to no good. They came to a stop in front of Florrie's house.

The girls stuck their fingers in their ears and wriggled them and hollered up to Florrie,

> *"Florrie, Florrie*
> *wets the bed,*
> *Florrie, Florrie*
> *Koo-Koo head."*

Florrie didn't seem to mind. She just laughed. But Molly was furious. "Rotten bums!" she yelled.

The girls turned to her and stuck out their tongues.

Molly went red with anger. "You both stink to high heaven!" she called, unable to think of anything worse.

"We're rubber and you're glue, what you say to us will bounce back to you," Celia said.

Florrie's mother appeared in the window.

"Lousy kids! Scram! Beat it!" she said. "Before I call the cops."

Celia and Beverly laughed, and ran across the street and into Celia's house.

Molly felt herself shaking as she sat down. She noticed Rebecca looking at her. She wondered what her little sister thought. Was she proud of Molly for talking back? Or did she think Molly should have done more? Molly won-

dered how she could have done more. Celia was mean. There was no telling what she might do. Besides, there were two of them and only one of her. She had yelled. That was something.

As she sat there thinking, Molly had to admit to herself that she was more afraid of Celia than she had thought. She had been acting like a big shot to cover up her fear. She had pushed the idea of a club, to force the other girls to help her. She was afraid to face Celia alone. She had known that before, but only as an idea. Now she knew it as a fact.

She didn't enjoy the feeling of being afraid. She told herself the only way to get over it was to face Celia alone. She decided to get the bracelet back without the help of the club. She glanced across at Celia's stoop. She would wait for Beverly to leave. Then she would go into Celia's hall and ring her bell. The thought frightened her. But she would do it anyhow.

Mama came to the window. "Molly, get Rebecca. It's going to rain any second," she said, and went back in.

Molly felt a few drops. She got down from her seat. "Rebecca!" she called, opening the hall door.

The people on the street began to rush to get home, but Rebecca just walked along. Molly wondered if her sister knew how to run.

"Hurry!" she called.

"I am hurrying," Rebecca said, coming up the steps.

"Do you know how to run?" Molly asked, closing the door behind Rebecca.

"What do I have to run for?" Rebecca said. "It's not a fire."

As the door opened and Joey came running in, Molly saw that the rain was splashing against the stoop with a fury. Joey was soaking wet. "Whew!" he said, pulling his wet shirt away from his chest. "I guess I didn't make it."

Thunder rolled across the sky and exploded, it seemed, overhead. Molly, Joey, and Rebecca looked at each other. Mama was in the house alone. She was afraid of thunder.

"Let's play cards with her," Molly whispered, opening the door to the apartment. "To take her mind off the storm."

They found Mama and Yaaki in the kitchen. Mama looked pale. Molly was sure Mama had just finished saying the prayer for protection from thunder, *Blessed is the Lord our God whose strength fills the world.*

Mama felt Joey's shirt. "You're all wet," she said. "Go change."

Molly had been through other storms with Mama. Mama did not like to play cards. But she would, if she thought she was doing the kids a favor.

"We hate to be stuck in the house, Ma," Molly said. "Come play cards with us."

Mama nodded, and Molly went to get the cards.

Thunder rolled across the sky.

"What do you want to play?" Molly asked, trying to talk louder than the thunder. "Come on, Rebecca," she said, sitting down at the table and making room for her sister.

"How about old maid, Ma," Molly said, knowing that would get a rise out of Mama. Mama had a lot of superstitions.

"Ptu!" she said, spitting the word away. "I don't want to play that game. And I don't want my daughters to play it either!"

Molly giggled. "Ma, we're too young to get married," she said, nodding toward Rebecca, to let Mama know she was only teasing.

"Even so . . ." Mama said.

"I want to play too," Yaaki said.

Joey came out of his room wearing dry clothes. He lifted Yaaki into the high chair. "What are we playing?" he asked, sitting down.

"So Ma, what do you want to play?" Molly asked.

Mama was silent as a clap of thunder sounded overhead. The rain pounding against the courtyard floor could be heard through the kitchen window. "Go fish," she said at last.

"Who's dealer?" Joey asked.

"The high card should deal," Molly said, holding the deck up to Joey.

Joey loosened a card from the deck. "Let Yaaki pick it out for me," he said.

Molly held the deck up to Yaaki and he pulled up the loose card.

"Eight of clubs," Molly said, reading it.

"Three of diamonds," she called, reading Rebecca's card.

Molly's card was the four of hearts, and Mama's the jack of hearts.

"Ma, you're dealer," Molly said.

"Joey, deal for me," Mama said, listening to the sounds out the window.

Molly handed Joey the cards and he dealt everyone a hand. They played game after game. Joey and Molly kept things lively, talking, kidding around, making dumb mistakes, all to keep Mama's mind off the storm. After a while Mama began to play seriously. Molly could see that Mama wanted to win.

"Hey, what is this?" Molly said, when Mama removed a queen from her cards to match the queen on the table.

"What do you mean?" Mama said, throwing down another card. She paused to listen to a roll of thunder overhead. "Play, Molly!" she said.

CHAPTER ELEVEN

The Bracelet

The thunder and lightning ended, but the rain continued all through lunch and into the evening. Papa
came home from work soaking wet. He changed his
clothes, and everyone sat down to supper; then listened
to the radio together.

The best program that night was Mayor LaGuardia.
Molly and her family loved him. He had a high voice,
and it got higher and higher when he was excited. He
told about how he had smashed a pinball machine that
day. He was against them because the gangsters owned
them. And boys were stealing nickels and dimes from their
mothers' pocketbooks to play the machines.

The next morning Molly nearly had a fit when she
opened her eyes. The room was as dark as night, and
the rain came down in buckets.

"It's still raining!" she shouted.

Rebecca, asleep in the same bed, woke with a start and began to cry. "Ma! Molly scared me!" she said.

Mama came running. She sat down on the bed beside Rebecca and held her. "You didn't have to yell," she said to Molly. "You scared her."

"Nothing scares her," Molly said, getting out of bed. "She's just saying that to get me in Dutch," she added, taking off her pajamas.

Yaaki came in.

Molly covered herself with her hands. "Ma, get him out of here—I'm trying to get dressed," she said.

Mama stared at her. "What's the matter with you?" she said. "He's only a baby." She took Yaaki by the hand and went from the room.

Molly turned to her sister. "Tell the truth," she said. "You weren't scared, were you?"

"I really was," Rebecca said. She crumpled up her face, the way she did when she was close to tears, and Molly knew she was telling the truth. She guessed she had been wrong, and she was sorry. She finished dressing in silence. The room grew lighter, and when she looked out the window, she saw that the rain was falling with less force.

"Ma," she said, going into the kitchen, "it looks like the rain is stopping."

Mama nodded as she glanced out the window. "Thank God. Now I'll be able to shop for *Shabbos*," she said.

"Where's Joey?" Molly asked, sitting down at the table.

"Where is he always? Out," Mama said.

As Molly sat sipping her cocoa, the rain stopped altogether. She heard people talking in the courtyard. She felt herself getting nervous at the thought of Celia. She listened for Celia's voice without really expecting to hear it. Celia's mother and the boarder would have gone to work. Celia had no one to talk to. But Molly was sure Celia was still up there alone, and maybe even looking out the courtyard window.

After breakfast, she hurried out. It felt good, stepping outside and being a part of the world, after being cooped up inside for so long. She reviewed her plan and changed her mind. Instead of ringing Celia's bell, she decided to catch Celia outside. It was too dangerous, being in the hall alone with Celia. There were always people in the street, and Molly could call for help if she needed it.

She sat down facing Celia's house. Florrie came out across the street and Molly waved to her. Molly kept herself erect, with shoulders straight, ready to spring. She was determined to make the day count.

Each time she saw Celia's door open, her heart jumped. But it was always someone else who lived in the building.

Mama came out, wheeling Yaaki's carriage. Yaaki and Rebecca walked behind her. Mama rolled the carriage down the steps of the stoop and stood on the sidewalk looking into her pocketbook.

"Molly," she said, "I forgot the ration card. It's on top of the refrigerator. Bring it, please."

Molly hated to leave her post. But she couldn't ask Rebecca or Yaaki to do it. They were too short to reach the top of the refrigerator.

"Watch Celia's stoop for me," she said, and ran inside.

Every family had a ration card. The government gave them out. Sugar, coffee, meat, and other things had become scarce since the war had started. People started hoarding those things, buying up piles at a time. The government put a stop to it by rationing, allowing each family to buy only so much at one time.

"Celia didn't come out, did she?" Molly asked, handing Mama the card.

"I didn't see," Mama said.

"No," Rebecca said. "I was watching."

Mama looked from Rebecca to Yaaki. "I forgot to ask. Did everybody go to the bathroom?"

"I did," Yaaki said.

"I went before," Rebecca said.

As her family went off, Molly sat down and once more took up her watch. Some time later, to her surprise, she saw Celia coming not from her house, but from the corner. Molly's heart raced as she watched Celia walk down the street. Celia didn't bother Florrie this time. Molly waited for Celia to get to the stoop.

"Celia!" Molly called as Celia went up the steps. She heard her voice shake and hoped Celia hadn't noticed.

Celia only looked at her. "Creep!" she said, and opened the door to go in.

Without thinking, Molly flew down the steps and ran into Celia's building. The narrow hallway was dark, but Molly saw Celia plainly at the end of it, near the stairs.

"Who said you could come into my hall?" Celia said.

Molly had to think fast. She didn't like being alone with Celia in the hall. She looked behind herself and saw that she could run out the door quickly if Celia tried anything funny.

"The bracelet belongs to Estelle," she shouted, a little too loudly, she thought. "Her mother hit her for losing it," she added in a softer voice, making up a lie. "Give it back to her."

"Who's going to make me, creep?" Celia said.

"Me," Molly answered.

"You and who else?"

Molly didn't know how to answer. She remembered her conversation with Mrs. Chiodo. "Your father!" she said.

Celia was silent. "My father's dead," she said after a moment.

"No he isn't. I know where he is, and so do you," Molly said.

Celia paused again. "Estelle gave me the bracelet."

"Is that why she was crying in my hall?" Molly asked.

"I don't know where I put it," Celia said.

"Yes you do," Molly said. She had felt Celia's toughness melting. She had said enough. It was now or never. She turned and opened the door. "Get it," she said. "I'll wait outside."

When she stepped outside, into safety, her blood began to rush. She was surprised. She had felt calm in the hall. Now, suddenly, she was shaking all over. She held the arm of the stoop and breathed deeply to steady herself.

She stiffened at the sound of the door clicking open. Celia might have returned with a bat instead of the bracelet. Molly watched Celia slam the bracelet down on the arm of the stoop and go back in without a word.

She picked up the bracelet and looked at the gold loop with little gold hearts. She felt a lurch of happiness. It occurred to her, as she turned to go, that she couldn't yet hand over the bracelet to Estelle. She didn't know where Estelle lived. Molly brought the bracelet into her house and put it on top of the refrigerator for safekeeping.

She felt quiet inside and wanted to hold on to the feeling. She went into Joey's room looking for a book to read. One sounded interesting: *Crime and Punishment.* She thought it might be about a person like Celia. She took the book into the living room and sat down to read.

CHAPTER TWELVE

Estelle's Joy

Molly quickly saw that the book had nothing to do with anyone like Celia. It took place in Russia, a long time ago. She had trouble getting into the story because the names of the people were too long.

The hall door opened and Mama came in with Yaaki, rolling the carriage. It was heaped high with grocery bags.

"*Oy*, thank God I'm home," Mama said. "The whole world was shopping, after the rain."

Molly put down the book. She began to feel a sense of excitement now that Mama was home. She went into the kitchen and helped Mama put the groceries away. She said nothing, waiting for Mama to spot the bracelet.

"What's this?" Mama asked as she put the milk away.

"What does it look like?" Molly asked.

Mama turned to Molly. "You got back the bracelet?"
Molly nodded, feeling pleased.

"Show me," Yaaki said.

Mama took the bracelet down and let him look at it.
She turned back to Molly. "You did a good deed," she
said. "Your friend, what's-her-name, will be very happy.
Why don't you bring it to her?"

"I don't know where she lives," Molly said. She felt
silly admitting it. She had gone to all that trouble for Estelle
and couldn't even say where she lived.

Mama took down an empty bowl from the cupboard.
"*Nu*, she'll probably be here soon," she said. She cracked
an egg into the bowl and beat it. "That was hard, what
you did, Molly," she said. "You should be proud."

"You and Papa did harder things," Molly said.

Mama had spread a clean cloth over half the table. She
put a wad of dough that she had prepared on the cloth
and began punching it. "What did we do?"

"Papa was in the army, in World War I," Molly said.

"And you came all the way to America from Palestine, without knowing English."

"I still don't know English," Mama said, kneading the dough into a ball.

Molly wanted to make Mama feel good. "Yes you do, Ma," she said. "You speak English fine."

"My English is still a baby," Mama said. "It needs to go to school."

Rebecca had come in from outside. "Is Molly picking on your English, Ma?" she asked.

"Nobody's picking," Mama said. "Look!" She nodded toward the refrigerator. "Your sister got back the girl's bracelet."

Rebecca looked up at the bracelet, then gazed at Molly. Molly puffed up at the look of admiration in her sister's eyes.

Yaaki pulled on Mama's dress. "Ma, I want music," he said.

"Molly, fix the radio for him, please. My hands are with flour," Mama said.

Molly went into the living room and switched on the radio. A faint sound could be heard. She turned the dial looking for music, and the strains of the song "Blueberry Hill" came up. She lifted Yaaki onto the couch, close to the radio, where he could hear the music.

"What do you say?" Molly asked her brother.

"Fanks," he said, listening.

Molly wondered why none of the girls of the club had come by. She guessed it had something to do with having been stuck in the house so long on account of the rain, and having lots of things to do outside today.

She sat at the kitchen table with Rebecca watching Mama roll the dough that had been rising. Suddenly the door opened and Estelle came in. Molly looked forward to Estelle's reaction.

"Hi," Estelle said. "Boy! How'd you like that rain, huh? My mother said it was like Noah's flood."

Molly, Mama, and Rebecca did not respond. They smiled at each other, waiting for Estelle to notice the bracelet. But Estelle only looked puzzled.

"What?" she asked, looking from one to the other.

"Look on the refrigerator," Mama said.

Estelle turned to look. Her mouth fell open. She took the bracelet. "How did you get it?" she asked Molly.

Molly felt important. "I just told her to give it back. That's all," she said, enjoying her role.

"Just like that?" Estelle asked.

Molly nodded.

"Boy! Wait till the club hears about this," Estelle said, slipping the bracelet onto her wrist.

Mama wiped her hands on a towel. "You know what, children?" she said. "This looks to me like a celebration.

And the Bible says a person should have candy for a celebration."

Molly knew her mother was kidding. "Where does the Bible say that?"

"Somewhere, I don't remember exactly," Mama said. She took a paper bag from the cupboard, shook some candies into a dish, and put the dish on the table.

"Come on, sit down, everyone," Mama said.

Rebecca stood looking at the candy. "Ma, that's the candy you bought for *Shabbos*," she said. "We can't eat it yet."

"*Shabbos* won't mind," Mama said. She nodded to Molly and Estelle to sit down.

"Come on, Yaaki, we're having a party," Molly called.

"I'm coming," he said, arriving.

Rebecca was still standing. "Ma, you told us not to eat candy before lunch. We didn't have lunch yet," she said.

"Is what?" Mama said, which was her way of saying *So what?* "Once in a while it's all right to make an exception."

"Rebecca, go close the radio, on account of the electricity," Molly said, helping herself to a candy.

Rebecca went to turn off the radio, then came back and sat down next to Yaaki.

"Where do you live, anyhow?" Molly asked Estelle.

"On Forty-fifth Street and Fourteenth Avenue, over the

grocery," Estelle said, sliding the hand with the bracelet across the table for a candy.

Mama asked Estelle about her family, and as they began to speak together, Molly heard voices from Celia's house outside, over the squeak of a clothesline that was being rolled across the courtyard. She listened.

"I don't think I should go," Celia's mother said.

"Come on—you'll have a good time," the boarder said.

"Yeah, but I really shouldn't . . ."

"Come on—it won't kill you. . . ."

"It's not fair to the kid. She's home alone a lot," Celia's mother said.

For a second Molly felt sorry for Celia. Then she remembered Celia's behavior with Florrie, and her old dislike for Celia came back. She popped another candy into her mouth. She was enjoying the way she felt. She had faced Celia alone. In her hall, where it was dark. It was a good feeling.

"Let's play cards," Rebecca said.

"How about old maid?" Estelle said.

Molly giggled as Mama brought the cards to the table.

"I'm not playing old maid," Mama said.

Molly laughed. "Ma, what do you care? You're already married."

"Never mind," Mama said, shuffling the cards. "I don't like that game. We'll play go fish."

"Me too, Ma," Yaaki said, wanting to play.

Mama dealt the cards. Mama helped Yaaki with his hand, Molly helped Rebecca, and Estelle helped Mama. There was no candy left in the dish when Estelle went home wearing her bracelet with the hearts.

CHAPTER THIRTEEN

An Ambulance Comes

Papa called on Mrs. Baumfeld's telephone to say he was working overtime, so Molly and her family sat down to supper without him. Afterward, Molly and Joey did the dishes.

"Who took my book *Crime and Punishment?*" Joey called from his room.

"I did," Molly said. "I thought it was going to be about something else."

"Just make sure you put it back," he said.

"Don't worry, I will." Molly knew she would not be reading any further in the book. She didn't have to read something she wasn't crazy about. Tomorrow was Friday, library day. She would be getting books she really wanted.

She headed for the door. Estelle had probably told the girls about the bracelet by now. Molly was sure one or

all of them would be showing up any minute. She could hardly wait to see their faces.

"I'm going out, Ma," she called.

Mama was reading the paper at the kitchen table. She looked up. "Keep an eye on Rebecca," she said.

"Ma, why do you always have to say that?" Molly asked. "Rebecca is outside right now. Nobody's eye is on her. Nothing happened to her."

"Ptu-ptu!" Mama said, making a little spitting sound, which was a way of saying *God forbid.*

"Why do I always have to keep an eye on her?"

"If you're outside and she's outside, what would it hurt you?" Mama said.

Molly couldn't think of an answer. She left without saying anything.

Outside, Rebecca was playing with Shimmy in front of his house.

Molly saw Little Naomi, in shorts, and the other girls running from the corner. They were waving frantically. Molly felt a flurry of excitement.

"Congratulations!" Little Naomi said, arriving first on the stoop.

Molly acted as if she didn't know what Little Naomi was talking about. "For what?" She stared at Little Naomi's legs. They looked twice as long in shorts. And her feet looked twice as big.

"Estelle told us," Little Naomi said, as Estelle held up

her arm and flashed the bracelet in front of everyone's face.

Molly was as happy as could be, but she tried to keep the smile on her face small so as not to seem to be showing off.

"You really got it back?" Lily said.

Molly nodded.

"I guess the boycott worked after all," Little Naomi said.

The boycott had had nothing to do with it. But Molly didn't want to say anything. She sat down on the stoop, and the other girls joined her.

"I was the first one to join," Lily said proudly.

"I was too," Lila said. "I was with you."

"Little Naomi was really first," Molly said, remembering.

Little Naomi grinned, as if she had won a trophy.

Estelle nudged Molly. "Look! There she is!" she whispered, gazing over Molly's shoulder.

Molly turned to see Celia looking at her.

"Sticks and stones may break my bones, but words will never harm me!" Celia hollered from her stoop.

"Who's talking about you?" Little Naomi called.

"Yeah, Miss Conceited!" Lily said.

Molly wanted them to stop. "Cut it out," she said.

Estelle made a megaphone of her hands. "Lower! Higher! You're . . ." she began.

Molly shoved her hands apart. "Come on, leave her alone," she said. "We got the bracelet back, didn't we?"

Suddenly the street froze into inactivity as an ambulance came screeching from the corner. The siren brought people rushing to their windows. Molly and the girls watched, waiting to see where it would stop. The ambulance drew to a halt in front of Florrie's house.

Molly felt her stomach tighten. "Gee, I hope it isn't for Florrie," she said softly.

She watched as two men leaped from the ambulance with a stretcher and ran inside. A few minutes later they came out holding the stretcher between them. Molly couldn't see who was on the stretcher, but she knew it was Florrie. Florrie's mother was behind it, walking and crying.

The men slid the stretcher into the back of the ambulance. Florrie's mother got in back with Florrie, and the men jumped in front and drove away.

The sight saddened Molly. She couldn't bring herself to speak. People left their windows. Everyone went back to what they had been doing, and the street returned to life.

Celia called, "You're stupid if you care. She's only a Koo-Koo," she said, and went down the steps, walking away.

Molly wondered if Celia was going to become a girl gangster, like her father, when she grew up.

Rebecca came walking up to the stoop crying.

"What are you crying about?" Molly asked.

"I don't want her to die," Rebecca said.

The same fear had gripped Molly. An ambulance was a scary thing. But she didn't want Rebecca to have to worry.

"Who said she's going to die?" Molly said. "People don't go to the hospital to die, they go there to get better," she added, wanting to believe her own words.

"Yeah, but she's sick. She *could* die," Little Naomi said.

"*Shhh*, don't say that," Molly said. "She won't die. We won't let her.

Little Naomi laughed. "Oh yeah? How are you going to stop it?"

Molly was sure there was something that could be done. "I'll ask my mother what Jews do when people go to the hospital," she said.

"Is Florrie Jewish?" Lily asked.

Molly had never given it a thought. She didn't know. Some Irish families lived around the corner. But on her block, everyone was either Jewish or Italian. Florrie had to be one or the other.

"Rebecca, go to Mrs. Chiodo and ask her what Italian people do when someone goes to the hospital," she said.

Rebecca sniffled and went next door.

"I'll be right back," Molly said, rushing inside.

She and Rebecca returned almost at the same moment.

125

"Well—my mother says Jews pray to God for the person to get well," Molly said.

Rebecca, coming up the steps of the stoop, said, "Mrs. Chiodo said the same thing."

"Let's pray," Molly said.

"Don't look at me," Little Naomi said with a giggle. "I don't know how."

"All I know is how to say *gut Shabbos*," Lily said.

"Me too," Lila said.

"Don't you have to go to a synagogue, or something, to pray?" Estelle asked.

"No," Molly said, thinking of the window in her room, God's window. "A person can pray anyplace. We'll pray right here."

"In front of everyone?" Lila asked, glancing around the street.

"No, in the hall," Molly said.

She opened the door, and the girls followed her inside.

"It's dark in here," Rebecca said, squinting.

"That's good—it's supposed to be," Molly said.

"What do we do now?" Estelle asked, giggling.

"Do we have to close our eyes?" Little Naomi asked.

Molly didn't think so. "Praying is the same as making a wish," she said. "You can, but you don't have to. I'll say the words. When I'm finished, you say *Amen*. That means you're in on the prayer too."

"But do we close our eyes?" Little Naomi asked again.

"If you want," Molly said.

"I'm going to close mine," Lila said. "Because if I see Lily I'm liable to laugh."

"What do we do with our hands?" Little Naomi asked, looking down at hers as if she had never seen them before.

"Everybody hold hands," Molly said, taking Little Naomi's hand. Each girl took the hand of her neighbors. They formed a circle. Molly thought it would be best if they all did the same thing.

"Let's all close our eyes," she said. When she looked and saw that all eyes were closed, she began.

"Dear God, Florrie, the girl who lives across the street, went to the hospital." She interrupted herself, regretting her words. God knew everything. There was no reason for her to explain. She hoped God wasn't insulted. She continued:

"Her mother is worried. So are the girls here in the hall, including me. We hope you will not let Florrie—" She had started the sentence wrong. She didn't want to have to say that word. She started over again. "We hope you will make Florrie better fast," she said, finishing.

She waited for the girls to say Amen, but they didn't seem to know it was over.

"It's over," she said, opening her eyes.

"Amen," they answered as they opened theirs.

CHAPTER FOURTEEN

Four More Weeks

Friday morning, Molly helped her mother get ready for *Shabbos.* Joey had changed the sheets on the beds and set up the cot for Aunt Bessie. Molly's job that Friday was to go around the kitchen with a bowl of soapy water, washing fingerprints off doors and walls. She liked working in the kitchen with Mama. The good smells of cooking and baking were strongest there.

Mama opened the door of the oven and removed a cake. The smell of cinnamon rushed out.

"Umm," Molly said, sniffing.

"Nu, thank God we have a cake for *Shabbos,"* Mama said.

"Why do you thank God, Ma? You made it yourself," Molly said as she put away the cleaning things.

"I only turned on the oven," Mama said. "God made

the plants in the earth that give us the food."

Molly took the pencil stub from the top of the refrigerator and opened the closet door to get at the calendar. She crossed off the week that had just passed.

Four weeks was still a long time away. But it was a lot better than five weeks, Molly thought. The idea that Tsippi's return was getting closer and closer warmed Molly.

"Four more weeks," she said. "Time flies," she added quickly, anticipating Mama's reaction.

"That's what I was just going to say," Mama said.

"I know," Molly said.

She went into the bedroom for the library books. As she gathered them up from the top of the bureau, her eye fell on God's window. She couldn't just look away. That would be rude; God might be watching. She didn't want to bother God about letting America win the war, or saving the Jews of Europe either. She had done that last night.

"Shalom," she said out the window, speaking the Hebrew word for peace, and left with the books.

On her way through the kitchen she saw Mama filling little triangles of dough with chopped meat.

"Oh boy! *Kreplach!*" Molly said, recognizing the meat dumplings that were being prepared.

"You guessed it," Mama said, pinching the corners of the dough together to seal in the meat.

130

"I'm going to the library, Ma," Molly said on her way to the door.

"What should I tell Lily and Shmilly and what's-her-name, if they come?" Mama asked.

"They won't come today. They help their mothers too. They'll come tomorrow," Molly said, and went out.

Molly saw Florrie's mother across the street and ran over to talk to her.

"How is Florrie feeling?" Molly asked.

Florrie's mother shrugged. She looked sad. "I just come from the hospital," she said.

"Was it on account of those two girls?" Molly asked. "Did they make Florrie sick?"

The woman shook her head. "No, they're bad girls, but they didn't do nothing. Besides everything else, she got diabetes, my poor Florrie."

Molly shuddered. It sounded like a terrible sickness, with the word "die" in it.

"Those girls," she said, trying to change the subject. "They don't act nice."

"She's a bad girl, that Celia. What do you expect?" she added, going up the steps.

Molly watched her go.

"Me and my friends prayed for Florrie," she called up.

The woman turned. "God bless you," she said, and went inside.

Molly found herself on the verge of tears as she walked away. She was touched by her own goodness. She let her eyes well up a moment, then blinked back the tears and walked on toward the library.

At Mrs. Pearl's suggestion, she took out *A Tale of Two Cities* by Charles Dickens. When she held the book, and saw how fat it was and how small the print was, she decided to take out only the one book. She didn't see herself reading more than one fat book that week. For Rebecca, she took out *Snow White and the Seven Dwarfs.*

Clutching her book happily, Molly thought about the club on her way home. The reason for starting it was over, but why not keep the club going? The thought excited her. Tsippi could join too, when she got back. As Molly thought more about it, she saw how easy it would be. They could keep the initials, and change the name.

The B, she decided, could stand for Brooklyn—all the girls lived there. The last C could stay the same—Club.

She needed to replace the middle C. "Children," she said to herself, trying out the word. She turned it down. The girls were grown up, and not children. Girls! By changing the C to a G, it could be B.G.C.—Brooklyn Girls' Club.

The idea made Molly happy. All her thoughts ran together and became one whirl of happiness. Florrie's mother had blessed her. Each day brought Tsippi's return closer. She had a new book. She would soon be sitting down to a *Shabbos* meal with the whole family. Aunt Bessie had a new green plate.

The wave of happiness that washed over her made her want to skip, and sing her happiness song. She wondered, since she was starting junior high, if she was too old to skip. *So what?* she decided. Holding the books fast, skipping along, she sang behind closed lips, so only she could hear:

> *"I should worry, I should care,*
> *I should marry a millionaire."*

jFic   cop. 1
C

Chaikin, Miriam

Lower! Higher! You're

a liar!